Leap of Faith

A Temporal Detective Agency Novel

Volume One

Richard Hardie

Discover us online:
www.authorsreach.co.uk

Join us on facebook:
www.facebook.com/authorsreach

Printed by Clays Ltd, St Ives plc

Leap of Faith is dedicated to all my family who, while I've been pounding the keyboard and counting rejection letters, never once told me to give up my hopeless dream.

The Author

Richard lives in the South of England with his wife, son and cocker spaniel. His daughter and her fiancé live nearby.

By necessity, he sells IT software, however by choice he write books for Young Adults. Twice a year, he goes to the Gower with his cocker spaniel and walks for miles along the glorious coastline. Amazingly, many plotlines arise during those trips and lots of plot logjams get freed up. It's a very cathartic time!

Richard was a Scout Leader for 15 years, during which time he wrote and helped produce five successful Gang Shows. That gave him a tremendous understanding of the humour and likes of children of all ages, and some of his characters are actually based on Scouts he knew, both girls and boys. His greatest influence (asides from the kids themselves) has been Terry Pratchett, who back in 2002 actually helped him write a scene for one of his Gang Shows and even acted in it..

Acknowledgements

As always there are too many people to mention, though I would like single out six people.

Four of them are my fellow authors in Authors Reach, all of who write far more books than I and to such a high quality that I'm continually amazed I'm part of their group!

Tracey Tucker's artwork inspired the original covers for my books and Gina Dickerson has taken over wonderfully. Her ability to interpret e a c h o f my stories into a single picture is incredible.

Some years ago I started working with a UK literary agent called Sarah (I won't mention her last name, though she'll know who she is). Sarah took the initial manuscript of what became Leap of Faith and, over a long period of time, told me exactly what I was doing wrong (many, many times!) and taught me how to write. Sarah told me to paste a piece of paper above my keyboard with the letters GOWTS on it. It stands for Get On With The Story, which is something many writers forget to do.

So before I break my own GOWTS rule, enjoy Leap of Faith, tell your friends about it and now Get On With The Story!

Richard Hardie
Eastleigh, Hampshire, 2013

Leap of Faith

A Temporal Detective Agency Novel

Volume One

A Bit at the Front

The Temporal Detective Agency

Camelot started to fizzle out when Arthur and the lovely Merlin went off to the island of Avalon for an extended honeymoon. Bless!

Okay, so Merlin was a woman… *Yawn!* …and the fantastic disguise I helped her with every day fooled the whole of Camelot for years, including a very confused Arthur. But that's another story and this one's about me and my friends in the Agency.

Let's start at the beginning.

The Knights of the rather worm-eaten Round Table drifted off one by one until there was no one capable of helping Arthur look after the country, and even my friend Galahad was too busy setting up his *Olé Grill* restaurant chain to be a politician. Of the others, Tristan moved to Cornwall and opened up a tea shop with scones to die for; Iolanthe, Bors, and Mordred were busy inventing a machine that could calculate; Gawain vanished one day on one of his adventures chasing the evil Black Knight; while others just got lost and were never seen again. I even heard

Guinevere went back to her father's place in North Wales with a besotted Lancelot hanging round her like a faithful puppy. To be honest there wasn't much point in staying round Camelot any more.

So we didn't.

The day after Merlin left, my cousin Unita (Neets to me), Marlene and I started the Temporal Detective Agency, opening for business in the wizard's old cave. We reckoned it was only right and proper considering we were Merl's last apprentices and Marlene was her younger sister. I say younger, but she was thirty if she was a day and getting really old and frumpy.

I suppose we could have moved to another part of Britain and opened up shop, but as we'd done a bit of time travelling with Merl and sort of inherited her Time Portal along with the cave, we decided to base ourselves in the twenty-first century where the cases promised to be more interesting than just finding missing pets. We also suspected the toilets would be much better than smelly holes in the ground half full of used leaves. We even persuaded Galahad to join us so we could use the *Olé Grill* restaurant as a cover and besides, he made great coffee.

What we found was that the sanitation and smells certainly improved, but the cases were still mostly dull because good, interesting crimes are few and far between, if not actually nonexistent. Business was pretty slow, but the retrieved felines kept Neets's cats company and the odd goldfish kept them from getting hungry. We even left business cards in carefully selected centuries knowing that *Temporal* would only mean *On Time* to most people. After all, who on earth really believes in time travel, but the only improvement was that we were asked to find a pet sabre-toothed tiger and the odd snake.

Neets and I thought it might be because we sounded a bit old-fashioned coming as we did from fifteen hundred years in the past, so Marlene enrolled us into college until we learned how to fit in and like rap music. No one knew where we came from, of course, but people seemed to sense we were slightly older than them by a few hundred years, and that can be quite off-putting to a young lad who thinks his luck's in. Still we did our best.

Nothing changed much, until one day…

Chapter One

Statues, Tunnels, Cellars and Knights

One minute I was munching on a bread roll in the twenty-first century *Olé Grill* and the next I was in London standing on top of Nelson's Column, spitting out crumbs like confetti at a baker's wedding.

That's a bloody awesome view! I thought, and it was. Then I looked down and thought *Oh piddle!* and I nearly did. I swore some more because Nelson's statue wasn't there and I was a hundred and fifty feet above the ground covered in pigeons. My legs turned to rubber and I lay flat out on the platform gripping its edges with my hands and feet as all sorts of gut-wrenching thoughts came to mind. Like, what if Nelson decided to make a sudden return and I got squashed? Like, what if no one noticed I was way up on the Column for weeks and I starved to death? Like, where was the bloody statue anyway and what was I doing replacing it? Like, there's never a spare pair of knickers around when you want them. And lastly … *HELP!*

Way below, a man was stammering through some sort of loudspeaker and I reckoned the odds were he was shouting at me. Gritting my teeth and fighting down the remains of the bread roll, I moved my arms and legs one at a time until I was in a sitting position as near to the middle of the plinth as possible. I gave a thumbs-up sign, though I don't know whether he saw it or not because there was no way I was going to look vertically down.

While things got sorted out below I chatted to the pigeons … anything to take my mind off where I was because four square feet is loads to dance around on when you're on the ground, but sweet nothing when you find yourself a hundred and fifty feet up in the air without a net.

The birdie conversation was getting a bit one-sided when a cage on the end of a long arm appeared with the loudspeaker man crouching inside. With my keen detective insight I could tell he wasn't at all happy with life, mostly because his face was green and he was being very sick.

"Hello." I probably said it too loudly considering he was only a couple of feet away, but his attention was definitely elsewhere. He opened an eye, looked at me sitting cross-legged in front of him and gagged. Okay, so I wasn't at my windswept best, I was wearing a robe covered in weird symbols, was in my low to mid-teens, and sitting exactly where Admiral Lord Horatio Nelson's statue had stood for more than a hundred and fifty years. But I'm not *that* bad looking for a time-travelling girl and yet the stupid man closed his eye again.

"Oi, you! Wake up." I clapped my hands because nobody goes to sleep when I'm talking, or I soon become their worst nightmare. "It may be a great view from up here, but it's bloody chilly. So if you'd be so kind as to open the gate on that box thing I'll join you and we can both return to solid ground." I carefully stood up, wobbled a bit to give the crowd below something to gasp at, took a short run-up and launched myself across the two foot gap, or to be more exact the one hundred and fifty foot drop into a sickening void, and grabbed the top of the cage. I swung inside and tapped the man on the arm.

"Hi, I'm Tertia from the TDA. What's your name?"

"Smollett." It wasn't all that clear because he was throwing up as he said it. I pitied those below.

"Just *Smollett*?"

"Inspector Smollett." It didn't look like he was

going to tell me his first name, not that I was really concerned because I knew enough about police ranks to realise that an inspector could make life very difficult. On the other hand, so long as we were suspended in the cage and the copper was losing his breakfast, I had the upper hand.

Inspector Smollett muttered something that sounded like, "Where's the bleedin' statue? You nicked it, we know you did. *Retch*. Where've you bleedin' hidden it? It'll go easier for you if you tell us. *Retch*." I ignored him because he was obviously delirious. Besides, I don't think his heart was in it and his stomach was certainly otherwise occupied.

"So, where do you come from, Inspector?" Small talk seemed a good idea. "Somewhere nice? Been on holiday this year yet? Did you fly?" The cage gave a lurch. "Sorry, wrong time to ask that. Still, you can see a lot from up here." I was standing by the open gate, holding onto the mesh roof with one hand and pointing to various buildings with the other. After the fright of the plinth I was beginning to feel a whole lot better. "What's that place?"

Inspector Smollett opened one eye. "Buckingham Palace." *Retch*.

"Nice! What's that one then?"

"Westminster Abbey."

I pointed at another.

"Houses of Parliament."

"Really? Looks different from up here. What're

9

those two big holes over there?"

"Marble Arch," he muttered. "Oh Gawd!" Any remaining colour disappeared from his cheeks almost as completely as Marble Arch had from Hyde Park. We both stared at Speakers' Corner where there were two perfectly good rectangular holes but definitely no arch.

I tapped him on the shoulder. "You can get up now, Inspector."

"I can't. You don't understand, I hate bleedin' heights." He wiped his mouth on his sleeve.

"I know and I do sympathise, but we're back on the ground and there are lots of people looking at you. People with notebooks and pencils mostly and some with cameras." I'd picked up a thing or two about journalists on my travels and already knew what the headlines would be on Monday morning.

Marble Arch disappears!
Leaves big hole in the ground!
Inspector Smollett says:
"Police are looking into it"!

I patted his hand, smiled and prepared to give my first ever interview. I turned to the reporters, gave a genteel cough, and began.

"Well, it all started like this…"

I decided not to tell the whole story. To be honest no newspaper in the world would have printed it and anyway my friends wouldn't have been impressed. That meant I had to leave out about ninety percent, but the rest was pretty good stuff and stubby pencils scratched away busily. All the time I was talking, Smollett kept pulling at my sleeve trying to interrupt and using the words loved by all coppers, *"You're nicked!"* I smiled at him sweetly.

As the last scribble ended, I took out an old metal cup and spoke into it, ignoring the thermos of tea and handcuffs offered by my inspector, as well as the astonished looks from the crowd of journalists. A muffled reply came from the cup and seconds later an ultraviolet archway materialised in the middle of the Column's fountain. It wasn't the most convenient of places, but with a wave and a smile I splashed into the arch followed by the inspector's increasingly distant voice: *"Stop in the name of the Law. Oh, bugger … where's she gone?"* and disappeared.

Zzzzzp.

Going through the Time Portal is a bit like flying through a tunnel … bloody narrow and best done in films. Looking back I could still make out the shrinking inspector sloshing around in the Trafalgar Square fountain trying to arrest a ghost and, at the other end, my friends were coming towards me like a train. I'd used the Portal loads of times, but when I ended up on Nelson's Column it was the first time I'd literally been sucked through it to somewhere not of my choosing. Come to think of it, I wanted to know where Nelson's statue had gone and whether Marble Arch's disappearance was a fluky coincidence. The copper obviously didn't think so and had me down as a statue and monument thief. I was well out of it and dead pleased to be on my way back home to the pleasures of a hot cup of tea and dry clothes.

It was then that things went all fuzzy as I shot off on a sort of temporal branch line and ended up sprawling on a cold stone floor. I lay very still in case I was on yet another column and slowly opened my eyes half expecting to see more pigeons, but it was less than twilight dark and there were no birds, just stuffy darkness.

I was in a room staring at a boy, which was a promising start. He was crouching down behind a mouldering packing case and mumbling what sounded like: *"Stop, stop! Oh, please stop! Lords above, what have I done? Oh, crap!"* He didn't seem in control of things and by the look of it I wasn't the only unexpected thing to have come out of the Portal. Damaged wooden boxes and smashed pottery littered the place while dust rose into the air as though there'd been a mini-explosion. After a minute of silence, the boy peeked out from behind his crate, inched forward on all fours towards a candle and swore as he burned his fingers on the still-smoking wick. He fiddled with flint and tinder and eventually managed to relight the candle stub.

The room was small with a solid-looking oak door,

had no windows and hardly any light to speak of other than the dim shimmer from the boy's candle and an unholy ultraviolet glow coming from the Portal archway. I never really liked that glow. The brick walls were bare and dripped with what looked like green slime, or really cheap hospital paint, but aside from the odd packing case and bits of broken crockery the room was empty and held nothing of interest except me lying on the floor covered in white dust.

The boy walked nervously towards the archway, ignoring me for some reason, and put out a hand to touch the switch that still glimmered to one side of the ultraviolet Portal. He pushed it up and dived full length across the cellar floor sliding to a halt by the door with his eyes shut and his hands over his ears. He probably thought the Portal was going to explode, suck him into some hellish netherworld, or slit his body down the middle and turn him inside out so his guts would slither over the floor like half-set red jelly. Which I suppose considering what had just happened to me and Nelson wasn't so crazy. All the boy got was silence as the Portal's whine wound down to a stand-by hum and the ultraviolet light blinked out.

He got up and by the remaining light of his candle stared at me as though he was trying to see if I were a statue, or just dead. I thought he was going to wet himself when I sat up, rubbed my eyes and said, "Where am I?" Understandable, I suppose. I coughed, beat at my robes causing billowing dust clouds, then held out both arms at full stretch as though magic were going to ripple from my fingers. He hesitantly approached again.

"Stay where you are, boy." I stood up and gave him a threatening prod with my forefinger. "One more step and I'll turn you into a rabbit. I can do that you know, because I'm a wizard. Or pretty well nearly a wizard." Amazingly the boy seemed to believe me, or at least he decided to stand back. "Tell me where I am and be quick about it. It doesn't do to keep Tertia, the nearly-wizard, waiting," I glanced at my clothes, "even when I look like a used duster. If you're going to open and close your mouth like a fish, then for pity's sake get some words out and answer my question." I looked around. "Okay, this is *not* Merlin's cave, or the *Olé Grill*, so where am I and what do you know about disappearing statues?"

I made the last words a stinging command and the boy sprang to attention although he managed to stop short of saluting me. "Y-you're *here*." He spread his hands wide. "You're in my father's cellars and we've no right to be here. He'll skin us both alive if he finds us down here, especially after what I've done." He looked as though he expected to hear his father's footsteps at any moment. "Honest, I don't know anything about statues. I only pulled a couple of switches and this devil's machine went mad. Things went flying round and all sorts of garbage got spewed out. Present

14

company excepted," he added quickly and very wisely.

So far I hadn't actually made any attempt to turn him into a rabbit and he was probably feeling slightly braver, so I decided to seize the initiative back. "Enough of your tomfoolery, boy. How dare you talk like that to a nearly-wizard member of the Temporal Detective Agency? I've a mind to teach you a lesson you'll never forget." Giving him the choice between an angry father and a vengeful me seemed to have the desired effect as a bead of sweat trickled down his forehead. "However, as you seem to know where I am and presumably how I got here I shall let you off and trust that your manners will improve. In consideration of my leniency, boy..."

"Bryn," the young man said quietly. "My name is Bryn, not *boy*."

I ignored his mumbled resentment. "...you'll tell me where we are and what you've got to do with Nelson's missing statue and Marble Arch."

Bryn looked at me suspiciously. "You're not from round here are you? I can tell. If you're from the Revenue and Excise the best thing you could do would be to jump back through that archway thing."

"I told you, boy," (there was a muttered *"I'm Bryn"*), "my name is Tertia. Actually I'm not sure if I did mention it, but it is," I waved dismissively as though names were unimportant, "and I have no interest in taxes of any kind. I try to avoid them like any sensible female."

"Oh, so you're a girl, then," said the boy called Bryn with remarkable insight, "which round here would make you quite acceptable if you weren't English and appeared out of my father's Time device. Personally, I've got nothing against girls, even if you do think you're a wizard and wear strange clothes. I'm quite open-minded and after all, this is the eighteenth century."

"Twenty-first," I said without thinking. "This is the twenty-first century. You've got to add a century onto the actual year, not take a couple away. A lot of ignorant people make that mistake." I was busy brushing dust off my robes when I noticed the look on Bryn's face, which roughly said: *I'm getting out of here. This girl's mad or I'm an Englishman!* I watched him edge back against the wall and realised almost too late that he was feeling his way towards the door.

"Where do you think you're going, young man?" I was watching Bryn like a one-eyed lizard. "Either you help me get out of here, or I take you with me through that infernal archway to whatever fate awaits us." I flicked the switch on the side of the Portal and spun a small wheel with numbers on it that made the thing hum. I smiled when the archway started to shimmer as the familiar whine reached a point just above human hearing and the ultraviolet pulsing glow throbbed into life. "Amazing! I'm not normally very technical. I usually leave things like this to my cousin. Now, boy, the decision is yours."

Before Bryn could answer we both heard footsteps approaching the cellar. They sounded strange. They weren't the confident steps of a man who knew he had every right to be there, but they sounded aggressively loud enough not to be friendly. "My dad!" Bryn sprang away from the door and grabbed me by the sleeve. "Are you really a wizard?"

I gave half a nod. "Apprenticed to the world's best. Merlin herself."

"Herself?"

"Long story."

"And you're really from the future?"

"If I'm from the twenty-first century and you're from the past then I must be in a way, I suppose. But originally I'm from long ago."

"You're mad! And you reckon you can change people into rabbits?"

"Well I exaggerated slightly there. That comes in year four with Merl I think."

"Then I'll come with you if I may. I like a bit of an adventure and if you're really a wizard where you come from it'll be more interesting than staying here and meeting my dad. You haven't seen him when he gets really mad. Actually neither have I, but after what I just did I don't want to, either." He shuddered and glanced at the door.

The footsteps had stopped and though I couldn't see it I sensed the handle was turning. Bryn grabbed my arm and hurried me towards the welcoming archway. "So tell me then, if you're not from around here, how come you're a female wizard dressed in those funny clothes and covered in dust?"

The handle was definitely turning now.

"Okay, if you want to waste time." I stood still and faced him with hands on hips. "Firstly these are my wizard robes, and secondly I was on top of a column somewhere in London and the next thing I knew I was here, for which it looks as though I can blame you. There was lots of dust up there, there's lots of smashed pottery down here and if you hadn't noticed I'm soaked up to my knees."

The door was inching open now.

"That's fascinating, Tertia," Bryn hadn't been paying attention to a word I'd been saying, focused as he was on his father. "I'd like to leave *now*, please."

I hung back. "You haven't told me where we are yet."

"Haven't I? You're in Port Eynon in South Wales in the year 1734..."

I uttered words like *"Blimey!"* and *"How the bloody Hell!"* which is most unlike me, because I know how to *really* swear.

"...and I strongly suggest we leave now." He pushed me into the archway and grabbed my hand. "I know my dad uses this thing so I know roughly what it does, but where are we going to end up? In the village square?"

As if I knew.

18

All he got in reply was, "Home I hope, but really I've absolutely no…" As we walked through the archway I glanced at the opening door and caught a fleeting look at the man entering the cellar. I recognised him instantly as a murderer, a fraud, a thief, and the man who ruined my parents and nearly killed them and half of Camelot. I thought he'd died centuries earlier when Sir Gawain defeated him, and I still hated him. I ran into the archway.

Zzzzzp.

Chapter Two

Case of Knights

I ran out of the Portal archway into the Temporal Detective Agency office and nearly fell over my own feet. Bryn tumbled after me, pointing at the archway and mouthing off about tunnels, infernal machines, and statues of wizards. Sweet boy.

"Get your cases packed, girls. We've got a bag!" I spat out the words. "I mean we've got a case. A real one, with real mystery and a real villain." Neets and Marlene stared at me open-mouthed because sometimes when I get excited I tend to forget people may not know what on earth I'm talking about.

"Come on in, dear," Marlene, the Agency's senior partner, was sitting on the edge of her desk looking powerfully dumpy. "Don't hang around dripping all over the floor just because your feet are wet. Take your shoes and socks off, grab a towel and dry yourself properly." The sister of the more famous Merlin watched as I got myself ready, then took the towel from me and threw it in a corner where I'd have to pick it up later. After all it was my turn for clean-up duty.

"Cup of calming Merl Grey?" Marlene poured me a mug of Merlin's favourite own-blend tea and sat down behind her desk. She arranged non-existent papers into a non-existent pile, then leaned back, pushing her fingers through her startlingly orange fright-wig of real hair. "Finished? Now, Tertia, tell me what happened and who this fine looking young man is. Then I'll decide if the Agency has a case or not." Marlene smiled at Bryn, who took a step backwards as though she'd sworn at him. "You know the rules about bringing home waifs and strays. Cats are one thing, but boys are definitely a *no, no*. By the way, I saw some of what you did through PortalVision, but the picture faded after you left the column. I have to admit I was worried for a moment and Unita was all for going to give you a hand, weren't you, dear?"

My cousin drew herself up to her full five-feet-eight inches, beating me by four. "I considered it for a second or two, but there's no way both of us would have fitted on that high pillar thing so I decided to stay here." Neets was a lot less impetuous than me, as well as being older by two whole years, and unlike me suffered from vertigo, whereas I only hated heights.

Bryn stared with his mouth wide open until our conversation ceased and we all looked at him, mostly with our arms folded. He shuffled his feet and gave a nervous smile, because after all he wasn't used to time travel let alone being in a room full of women who assumed they were in control and thought they could turn him into a rabbit.

"I would still like to know who this young man is, Tertia," said Marlene, pressing her question, "and why on earth you decided to bring him with you. I would also like to know more about this wonderful case and especially about your incredible villain."

"I couldn't leave the boy there, could I?" I said. "I mean, I saw the man and from what Bryn said I reckon he must be his dad." I tried the ultimate objection. "I bet you and Neets would have brought 'im ... being sensible adults. Anyway, it was definitely 'im!" I was still excited, in spite of the Merl Grey tea.

"She didn't bring me," Bryn said without much conviction, "I brought myself. I'm quite capable of making my own decisions, you know. Besides, I like my dad. It's just that this time I did something really stupid and he'll skin me for it."

"You may be right, Tertia," said Marlene, totally

ignoring Bryn. "If we're to find out what happened to Nelson's Column, Marble Arch, and you, it looks like the lad could be very much involved, if not the unwitting cause." She emerged from behind her desk and started pacing like Sherlock Holmes, but without the pipe and violin.

"Hang on," I said indignantly. "I'm the one who was sucked through space and time. It's me that got landed on top of a column. It was me that got shoved into a cellar with this lad. It was me that ruined a perfectly good pair of shoes in that water fountain and it was me that saw the man." I felt people were ignoring my last point. "*The Man!*" I repeated just to reinforce it.

"A case worthy of the Agency, I admit. No missing pets to find for a start." Marlene stopped pacing up and down her office and perched on the edge of her desk. "Actually, which man are you talking about?" I stared at her and continued to drip on the carpet, while Bryn stared at all three of us with his mouth agape and probably wished he were back home. If I had my way he soon would be and if Marlene had hers he wouldn't have left in the first place.

"The Black Knight, that's who!" I was nearly shouting. "The bastard that tried to murder my parents and nearly killed Merl and Arthur. He was in Bryn's place."

Marlene gave an adult's superior smile. "It can't have been him, Tertia. Arthur had the Black Knight

23

executed after Sir Gawain defeated him, so how could he have been in South Wales, let alone in the year 1734?"

I mouthed a few expletives of frustration and Neets came to my rescue.

"We didn't *actually* see him die," she reminded us. "We were just *told* he'd been executed. If Tersh saw him at Bryn's place maybe he didn't die."

"She's right," I said. "What if the bastard escaped from Camelot? He had enough supporters inside the castle and I bet Arthur wouldn't have boasted about it. Let's say he did get away and got to South Wales through a Time Portal."

"Impossible," said Marlene. "There are only two Portals, ours and the spare back in Merlin's old cave in Camelot. And that one doesn't work anymore," she looked thoughtful, "unless of course Merlin kept others for spare parts in her old castle workshops. It's quite possible, knowing my sister."

"But we know there's another Portal, Marlene." I pointed at Bryn. "I saw it in the boy's cellar and we used it to get back here. That means someone from Camelot must have taken it to South Wales and as I saw him plain as day it must have been the Black Knight." I looked at the boy who had hardly moved since we'd arrived. "Is that evil man your father, Bryn?"

Bryn stiffened. "My dad's my dad! He's not evil." I don't know why I'd expected him to do anything but defend his father. After all I'd have done the same, except of course that my dad had been a farmer and was nearly killed by the Black Knight. "He does the odd bit of smuggling like everyone," Bryn continued. "The odd barrel of brandy, some bales of silk, and a few crates of tea, but he'd never hurt anyone and he's not even a bit bad really. Who is this Black Night anyway?"

I reckoned Bryn deserved an explanation, but Marlene beat me to it. "Back in Camelot... *I take it he knows about Camelot?*" I nodded, "...the Knights of the Round Table looked after King Arthur and protected his kingdom. One of them, called the Black Knight – they all had silly names – wanted Guinevere and the kingdom for himself and tried to kill Arthur and take over Camelot. He nearly did it too, because lots of the best Knights had either retired, or were off on stupid quests. Only Sir Gawain, the White Knight, had enough sense to get together a band of soldiers and attack the Black Knight's small army before it reached the walls of Camelot, but unfortunately not before it laid waste to most of the farms and villages and killed many of the peasants. Unita's and Tertia's parents got away with their lives, but everything they owned was destroyed. The Black Knight was captured by Gawain and taken to Camelot castle and was only seen once after that, when we all thought we saw him executed. Now it seems he may have escaped and somehow may be your father."

"That's crazy!" said Bryn with a splutter and I had to admit I wanted to agree with him, except I'd seen the proof with my own eyes. The man coming into the cellar had definitely been the most hated man in Camelot.

"That murdering bastard's behind all this, I know he is, and we certainly can't send Bryn back alone to a father who's a murdering bastard." I paused. "Marlene, we have to go back there with him. The Agency has to go and sort this out, statues and all."

Marlene ran her fingers through her shock of flaming ginger hair. We looked at her expectantly, because quite honestly there was nothing else for us to do. "If you're right then I agree it's almost certain the evil thug's behind it all and we have to do something about it. But there are things you don't know yet. Like what exactly is that statue doing in the middle of the *Olé Grill?*"

Marlene slid off the desk and led us out of her office into the restaurant's dining area which, because it was Sunday morning, was empty. In the middle of the room and surrounded by tables was an over-sized conversation piece that was beyond words. Well, mine anyway. It was definitely made of stone, looked extremely well-weathered and as a statue was vaguely familiar.

Neets walked up to it and examined the figure like an expert. "If I didn't know better I'd say this was

26

from Trafalgar Square. Not that I've seen it up close of course, just from photos. It's about the right height and a very good copy." She walked round the statue. "So good in fact, it's covered in pigeon droppings."

"What, you mean real ones?" I asked, getting interested.

"Want to taste some?"

I wasn't sure if Neets was serious, but I shook my head anyway.

Marlene coughed. "I don't believe in coincidences," she said. "Nelson's statue being swapped for Tertia, Tertia ending up in South Wales in 1734 then coming back here with the boy through an illegal Portal, Marble Arch completely disappearing, and behind it all it looks as though we've got the Black Knight in the wrong country let alone the wrong century, way after he should have died. Interesting, don't you think?" Marlene had a massive grin across her face. "Like Tertia said, we've got a case to solve and there isn't a missing pet in sight. The Temporal Detective Agency is in business and we've got a real villain to bring to justice." She looked thoughtful. "The fact is though, girls, we're still amateurs and need a professional to get us on the right track." She marched back into her office and fiddled with the sleeping Time Portal's mass of knobs and dials, while Neets and I looked on in puzzlement. Bryn still sat in Marlene's chair looking understandably dazed and trying not to be noticed.

Marlene thrust her arm into the archway and we watched it disappear until only her shoulder was left. She was obviously blindly searching for something and from the intense look of distaste on her face it could well have been down the S-bend of a toilet. She gave a grunt of satisfaction and pulled as hard as she could as a terrified inspector Smollett sailed through the Portal, landing face down on Marlene's desk, water pouring from his shoes onto the carpet and adding to the pool I'd created earlier. Of course his feet were several times larger than mine so he dripped longer and more thoroughly.

Marlene pursed her lips and examined the inspector with detached interest. "Girls, this is our professional," she walked up to her desk and prodded the trembling figure, "though he looks more like a wet fish and I'm inclined to throw him back."

Smollett was lying on his stomach, but managed to shake his head vigorously.

Marlene patted him on the shoulder. "Don't take on so. Do you really think I'd have gone to all the trouble of bringing you here, not to mention getting another soaking for my carpet, just to send you away with a flea in your ear?" She laughed and gave him a none-too-gentle shove. "Come on, get off my desk and take off your shoes and socks. Tertia, pass him your towel, dear. It's in the corner over there."

Inspector Smollett did as he was told and pushed himself into a sitting position on the edge of the desk.

I handed him my towel and grinned. "So we meet again, Mr Inspector Smollett, and while I've got the chance I suppose I ought to say thank you for getting me off that pillar thing, even though you were trying to arrest me for the theft of a statue. I was getting a bit bored up there. Great view and all that, but when you've seen one vertical drop you've seen them all." Smollett winced and I suspected anything over six feet made him feel sick and that included his own body wearing four-inch stacked heels. Smollett dried his feet on my towel and tried to squeeze as much water as possible out of the bottom part of his trousers.

Neets turned to Marlene. "Nice person I'm sure, but I don't see how he's going to help us. He's just a copper."

"But that's the point," explained Marlene as though that said it all. "Mysteries like this are bread and butter to guys like him." Smollett was shaking his head now and trying to mouth the word *No!* but none of us took any notice. "You'll see, he'll take to this little lot like a duck to water." She looked at the pool spoiling her treasured carpet. "Besides, he was close to hand when we wanted him."

"A bird in the hand ... usually makes a mess all over your palm," I said, but no one laughed.

Marlene took Smollett by both hands and pulled him upright, partly because he didn't look as though he could do it by himself, but mostly because I knew that sitting on the edge of her desk was her privilege and anyone else doing it was taking a liberty. She patted him on the shoulder, smoothed his hair, and adjusted his tie like the concerned mother of any schoolboy.

"There you are," she said with a final flourish and pecked him on the cheek, "as good as new." She clapped her hands. "Now, I'd like to get this detective agency doing what it's supposed to do. Let's go and solve Tertia's mystery!"

Neets saw the only flaw in the whole thing; who exactly was going to pay us? But as we hardly ever got paid, even as a flaw it was flawed. Besides, anything we made would now have to be split between Marlene, us two girls from Camelot, a very confused young lad from some Welsh seaside village we'd never heard of, and a London detective with a terrible head for heights. I could have included Neets's cats as a back-up, but Galahad would have made a better reserve on the basis he didn't leave unpleasant surprises in the corner unless they were chargeable plus tax.

Inspector Smollett was the first to comment by leaping to his feet and making a run for the restaurant's cave entrance. Dodging round the tables he slipped, bounced off Nelson's statue, tripped over my outstretched leg and landed in a heap in front of the smiling Galahad. The knight gently picked him up and led him back to Marlene's table like any good restaurant owner with a client who hasn't paid yet.

30

Smollett turned to me, looking like a startled rabbit. "I arrest you for the theft of this statue and me as well," he squeaked and I almost felt sorry for him.

"Don't be silly," said Marlene in a suddenly very businesslike voice.

The detective looked around nervously as Galahad smiled, watching the inspector who without thinking was nibbling on a small bread roll. The knight told me once that he found people tend to get a weird thrill from experiencing any outrageous charge, especially when they're not actually going to have to pay it. I reckoned my inspector was munching on a theoretical fiver at least.

"Can I go, please?" Smollett muttered through a mouthful of crumbs.

Marlene gave him a guilty smile. "Sorry, Inspector, I'm afraid I need your help. The facts are one thing, but I need your deductive powers as a copper and who knows, I might even need to borrow your handcuffs depending on how we get on."

Smollett sat down and finished off his vastly expensive roll. I reckoned it could now be a tenner from the look in Galahad's eye.

Marlene looked at me and tapped her chin again. "Tertia, when you left the cellar was Bryn's father in the room? I mean, I know you saw him, but could he see you? Think now, this is important."

I thought long and hard. "Yes … he'd just come through the door when we disappeared."

"And the Portal was still switched on when you left?"

"Yes." I wasn't sure where this was going.

"So Bryn's father could follow you here just by looking at the Portal dials and seeing where they were set to."

"Oh yes!" I saw where this was going, got up and padded in my bare feet into Marlene's office, avoiding the stubborn pools of water. The familiar whine started up as the dull ultraviolet glow lit the small room when I switched on the Portal and with great care studied the dials, checked some numbers, made fine adjustments, then crossing the fingers on one hand, slid the other into the shimmering archway. I felt around and with a smile of satisfaction, found what I was looking for and spun the dials three seconds after Bryn and I left so that no one on the Welsh side would know where we'd gone and be able to follow us to the agency's cave, especially the Black Knight.

When I returned, Marlene picked up a small travelling case and handed it to me, together with a small remote-control box. "Right, get packed, girls. You're going to the seaside. I'm sure Galahad will lend you some clothes, Inspector. Bryn, you look fine as you are. Personally I'm staying here to coordinate things."

I glanced at Marlene wondering if I'd heard right, but she was whispering urgently to Bryn. It wasn't like her to take a back seat, but I presumed she had her reasons and I didn't ask what they were.

Galahad reset the tables and patted Nelson's statue for good luck, then disappeared through the Portal to open up the *Olé Grill* restaurant in all the other centuries where he had a franchise. Before he went, I saw him look under Marlene's saucer by force of habit for a non-existent tip.

Half-an-hour later, four figures disappeared through the Time Portal. Bryn wasn't looking forward to going home, Neets asked why I was taking suntan lotion to work, and Smollett knew his Sunday lunch was ruined.

Destination ... Port Eynon in 1734.

Purpose ... to solve the statue mystery and beat the evil Black Knight.

Big bonus ... no dull cases like missing cats and dogs.

Zzzzzp.

Chapter Three

Cellars, Towers and Vicars

"Tersh," Neets said quietly, "you remember when we turned up in the Sheriff of Nottingham's dungeons and were in pitch darkness with the skeletons?"

"Yes, looking for his bloody cat," I whispered back. "Why?"

"You don't think we've landed back there, do you? Wherever we are has a tremendously unlit dungeonish feel." Unita bumped into me blindly coming the other way and gave an ear-splitting screech before recognising me by touch and my own scream.

"Where's Smollett, Neets?" My heart had returned to something like normal speed. "Come to that, where's Bryn?"

"Damn!" said a Welsh voice from floor level. "I know I dropped it somewhere round here." There was the sound of scrabbling and scratching. "You could help me, unless you're too proud and ladylike to get your hands and knees dirty where you come from? Oh, I forgot you were both born in Camelot." There was more mumbling and then a grunt of satisfaction. "Got it. You can stay where you are, your highnesses. I've got everything in hand." After several seconds there was a sudden searing flash of light, which soon dimmed down to the guttering glow of a candle stub.

"Bryn, is that you?" Neets called out stupidly.

"Of course it is. Who else would it be?" Bryn snapped at her. "And keep your voices down, or you'll have my dad on our backs."

"Are we in your cellar then, Bryn?" continued my *very* clever cousin Neets.

"Duh … of course we're back in my father's cellar," he said trying to imitate Neets's voice, but so badly that none of us noticed. "That was always the point, wasn't it, to come back here?"

"Yes, of course," Neets rallied. "It's just I've never been here before and Tertia was only here for a few minutes before your father nearly caught her." She looked around. "It's just a room with some crates in it, like you said, Tersh. Dingy, dusty and cellary."

"And one we need to get out of pretty darn quick," I added, "or being found by the Black Knight may become an end-of-a-lifetime experience."

Smollett was sitting in the corner of the cellar staring at nothing and having what sounded like a losing argument with himself. He also had a worryingly silly smile on his face that had nothing to do with humour. I prodded him with my foot. "We need your copper's flashlight, Mr Inspector. I know you've got one." He didn't look at me, but at least he stopped the mumbling. I dug around in his pockets and found a small pencil torch. "Are you okay Mr Inspector?" I shone the light in his eyes and decided it was only a bit of delayed time-travel shock and there wasn't much wrong that a good slap wouldn't put right. Smollett leaped to his feet and pointed at the pulsating Portal archway, spluttering words that involved a deep knowledge of swearing and flecks of spittle, so I slapped him again for good measure. "Pull yourself together, man. Anyone would think this was your first trip in time."

"You hit me." Smollett sounded almost normal, at least for a time-travelling copper. "I arrest you for kidnap and assaulting statues."

"Shut up and follow me." It was as good as a third slap.

"Fair enough, but can I have my flashlight back, please." My inspector seemed to have got over his temporal shock as I handed him his light, and he meekly followed me.

Neets had ignored my conversation with Smollett and was more interested in watching her Welsh boy wonder who in turn was more interested in listening for his evil father. Bryn walked up to the cellar door, but stopped just as he reached it. "We didn't think. My dad's bound to have locked the cellar after we left. What do we do now? Go back?"

I pushed past him with an exaggerated huff. "Boys!" I turned the handle and opened the door, which hardly gave a squeak. "People don't think to lock doors after the event, only before."

"I was about to do that," Bryn protested. "Honest. Anyhow, that door always squeaks when my dad opens it and it certainly did when I tried it earlier, so how come it opened quiet as a mouse for you?"

"Because I open a door as though I really mean to open it." I swung the door a few times to prove my point. "Not so slowly that it's almost an apology. Doors are like boys; they appreciate authority. Remember that, Neets." I walked out into the corridor linking the cellars, followed closely by Smollett who probably had no idea what to make of me, then made my way up the stairs leading to the ground floor.

"How on earth did you know it was open, Tersh?" Neets followed close behind, dragging a reluctant Bryn by the arm.

"I didn't." I was near the top of the stairs and was

very slowly opening a door that presumably led to the hall. *Squeak!* "But I reckoned it was a good bet that Bryn's dad wouldn't have locked it. After all, we'd disappeared so what was the point. Never lock a door if you don't *really, really* have to and especially if there isn't an intelligent woman nearby to tell you to do it. It's a man thing, Neets." I paused as I looked up and down the hall to make sure the coast was clear. "And of course I guessed. But don't tell Bryn, he'd be so disappointed. He thinks I'm wonderful!"

A fit of coughing and the sound of male shins being kicked told me that Neets and Bryn were just behind me. I smiled because Bryn wasn't all that bad looking in a hunky sort of way if you forgot how thick he was. And he didn't seem to mind that in theory Neets was more than a thousand years older than him. *Perhaps he likes older women* was my last thought before Neets caught up with me.

"All clear?" Neets was peering over my shoulder. "Bryn reckons nobody'll be around at this time of day. All the servants will be out and his father doesn't usually come into this part of the house unless he's going to the cellars."

I considered all this and shook my head. "What a load of bunk. How on earth can he know the time? Sundials in cellars are as useful as an ice frying pan. He's trying to impress us just like any boy with a crush."

"I can tell from the angle of the sun coming

38

through the window," said Bryn with what could have been a sneer. "It's late morning, probably about a quarter to twelve, so all the servants will be in the Sunday morning service, as will my father. It'll be finished soon." He sounded as though he should have finished with a *Nah!* but he didn't.

"What makes you think it's Sunday, smart guy?" I pressed, peering out the cellar doorway into the hall. "It could be a Wednesday for all we know. Just because you and I left here on a Sunday doesn't mean a thing as Marlene would tell you if she were here."

"I know it's Sunday," Bryn said smugly, "no shadow of a doubt … smart girl!"

"There's a calendar on the wall over there and it definitely says it's Sunday," added Neets meekly, pointing to the opposite wall. "Sorry, Tersh, but he's right."

"I knew that!" I said a little bit too loudly. "I just wanted to check. So, coast's clear and we can go. I don't know what you two are waiting for, but I'm parched. I'm going to find somewhere I can get a drink and something to eat, then it's down to work with my inspector. That is if you two have quite finished messing around trying to prove how clever you are." I was in a huff, and as huffs go this was quite a good one.

"Master Bryn!" A door at the other end of the hall opened and a boy about Neets's age stared at us in horror. "You're not supposed to be here. I mean, I thought you were out at church." He looked really flustered.

Bryn looked with equal horror at the boy. "David! I thought you'd be in church too." He turned to Neets. "He's our kitchen boy. Don't worry, he's dead stupid. He won't say anything."

"Will that be two extra guests for Sunday lunch then, master Bryn?" asked the stupid kitchen boy with what seemed to me to be a most sensible question. I could have devoured a good roast in minutes.

Bryn put a finger to his lips. "Shush, David. This is a secret and you mustn't tell anyone we've been here. Nobody, you understand? Not even my father." The boy's face broke into a stupid grin.

Especially not his bloody father, I thought.

Before Neets could object, Bryn took her by the hand and marched through the hall and out the front door into the world of 1734. I trailed behind and in spite of myself couldn't help feeling that for someone as cruel and nasty as Bryn's father, this really was quite a nice house. It was airy and for some reason the word *cheerful* came to mind. Through the stained-glass windows the sun made colourful patterns on the floor and the whole effect looked intentional, as though someone had gone to a great deal of trouble to create a feeling of calm. It wasn't the sort of place you would expect a murdering thug to want to live. Back in Camelot my original home had been an old farmhouse with no heating or running water and the place had been destroyed by the Black Knight soon after I joined Merlin. In comparison Bryn's house was to die for and if his father had his way that's probably what would happen. I hurried after the other two.

As we walked down the mansion's driveway, I glanced to my left and saw a tall heavily built figure riding a horse as though he were fighting it rather than enjoying the experience. He stopped at the top of the road leading into the village and stared at us as we made our way down the lane towards the bay and even at that distance I could see the look on his face was one of disbelief and hatred, mostly hatred. I admit I wanted to hide as he pointed at me and sneered. He wiped the sweat off his forehead, pushed his long, lank hair out of his eyes and savagely pulled back his horse's reins making it rear onto its hind legs, before galloping round a bend at the top of the road. The Black Knight had never liked horses. I grabbed Bryn's arm, but by the time I had his attention his murderous, hairy thug of a father had disappeared.

We walked on, because there was nothing else to do under the circumstances and our arrival was no longer a secret. Splitting up always seemed to work in Hollywood, a place I thought one day would suit an outstanding talent such as mine, so I decided to take my inspector and explore the village, while Neets followed Bryn through the village towards the Salt House.

41

"We need to find a library if they have such a thing," I said as Smollett fell into a copper's stroll beside me. If he was still suffering from the horrors of time travel he wasn't showing it and Bryn seemed to be handling the whole thing like a veteran. But then he had a father who was a seasoned traveller and that undoubtedly helped.

"Or we could have a look at the church archives," Smollett suggested.

"Or we could look at the church archives," I muttered. "I was just going to say that!" I hate people being one guess ahead of me when I'm on a guessing roll.

"In my spare time I'm a keen genealogist." My inspector added by way of explanation.

"I don't care if you are a part-time doctor. We're here to find out about *people*. I want to know when the Black Knight actually arrived and why he chose this place."

Smollett shot me the look of a perplexed puppy, but remained silent.

The church was halfway up a hill leading out of the village and the building itself probably hadn't changed for hundreds of years. The grass in the graveyard was kept tidy by a small flock of sheep; so much quieter than noisy mowers ruining a restful Sunday afternoon snooze. I banged on the church door.

"There's no need to knock," boomed a voice from behind us. I jumped a foot into the air beating

Smollett by several inches and nearly knocking him out. "We're always open to people who wish to visit for whatever reason. Many come here for our brass rubbings, others like to make a small donation towards the church restoration fund." A small collection tin appeared miraculously out of nowhere and hovered under our noses. "On the other hand maybe you want to book my church for your wedding?" said the voice hopefully. "We haven't had a good wedding for some months now. Though looking at you both ... perhaps not."

The vicar was seven-foot-six ... well, at least six feet and had the body of a well-built gorilla. He was totally bald, without even eyebrows, though he did have a bushy beard that hid the lower part of his face. He had a ruddy complexion and the wicked grin of a man who enjoys life and knows he shouldn't. Even his clothes weren't those of a vicar and he looked as though he'd just returned from a long walk to the pub. With a smiled apology he leaned over me and pushed the doors open with what looked like the flick of a finger.

"Come on in," said the vicar, his voice louder than a megaphone and very, very Welsh, "come on in and tell me how I can assist you." He led the way inside and sat on a pew in the small church's central nave. "I'm sorry I can't offer you anything more comfortable, but as you can see this is hardly a cathedral and we have very few amenities. Though of course a donation…" The tin appeared again and was rattled suggestively. Smollett automatically reached into his pocket, but mumbled an apology as he pulled out a handkerchief and blew his nose. The tin disappeared and we sat down. "Please excuse my clothes." He must have seen me looking at his lack of vicarish attire. "I went for a walk after the morning service to clear my head."

"Vicar, we need your help." I peered closer at the bald gorilla. He looked vaguely familiar. "I take it you are the vicar? You can't be too sure these days … or any days for that matter."

"I know what you mean," said the bearded giant. "It's amazing the sort of people you get in here. I see all manner of confounding things and hear all kinds of weird stories. And now I hope I'm going to hear yours." He crossed his legs, folded his arms, and leaned back in his chair with a comfortable smile. Had there been a cup of tea nearby he would have sipped from it, though probably not with his arms folded. "I'm waiting."

The giant of a man stared at me for a full half-minute as though trying to come to some weighty decision, then threw back his head and laughed. Tears were wiped away with a small lace hanky that I couldn't help feeling looked rather out of place when used by such a powerful man, and in a church.

"This?" The vicar saw where I was staring and held up the lace handkerchief which had the initials **GP** monogrammed in one corner. "Oh, I know it looks strange, but it was a present from an old friend of mine and I suppose it has sentimental value. Let's face it, as a vicar I don't have many material possessions and it's only for a bit of show." He put the handkerchief away with a flourish.

"Thank you, Mr Vicar."

"Call me Illtydd. Named after the saint."

"Okay. Ill Ted," I said. "Sorry to hear you're not feeling well. Anyway my friend here is very much into local history."

"Well, why didn't you say so," Ted the vicar offered with enthusiasm. "I've been here now for more years than I care to remember and have made a special study of the village's history. What would you like to know? Go on, ask me anything." Ted closed his eyes and waited with an *I know it all, test me, test me* smug look on his face.

"Well, Mr Ted," I said it very quietly because we were in a church. "I want to know everything about a certain Mr Lewis. I believe he's a smuggler amongst other things. My friend on the other hand," I pointed to the inspector trying to involve him somehow, "is interested in architecture."

"I'll see what I can do," mused Ted. "The name Lewis is very familiar to me, after all it's one of the most common names in Wales and I also happen to be a Lewis. There's one though that might interest you. He's a nasty piece of work; a notorious smuggler, murderer, and ship wrecker by all accounts." I looked at my inspector triumphantly and mouthed the words *our Black Knight*. "As for architecture, come with me and I'll show you what we have from an ideal viewpoint."

Motioning us to follow, Ted strode towards the far end of the church and opened a small door that allowed one very small person to enter at a time. Even I had to bend down to avoid cracking my skull, which meant that Ted looked like a cork desperate to get back into a bottle.

The tower was no more than forty-feet high, but because the church was on a hill the view overlooking the village was spectacular and I was becoming an expert on views by now. I walked to the tower's low wall from where I could see every building in the village itself and for a mile either side on the coast. Ted joined me while Smollett hung back by the entrance to the spiral staircase and pretended to scan the horizon, crouched down with eyes closed.

"I take it your friend doesn't like heights," observed Ted. "It's going to make it difficult showing him the important buildings he wants to see."

"Never mind him." I gave Smollett the most fleeting of glances and tugged at Ted's sleeve. "He'll be fine. Tell me all about what's down there and I'll fill him in later." In more ways than one, I thought. A fat lot of good Smollett was proving as the professional lead detective. "So what have we got?" I hoisted myself onto the wall and leaned on my arms to get a better view.

"Do be careful." Ted put a hand on my shoulder. "Accidents happen and we've had one or two people fall from up here in the past."

"It's amazing," I said, totally ignoring the warning. "The way it's all laid out like a map. You almost feel you could fly."

"That's the temptation," said Ted tightening his grip on my shoulder. "Please resist it if you can."

"I'm fine thanks." I shrugged off his hand because I had the strangest feeling it was either there to hold me back or push me.

"Over there to the left," Ted pointed, "is the public house where they serve strong liquor to people with weak spirits. Sorry, that was a vicar's joke! The place is very old and I believe they have rooms for the night if you're interested. Way over to the right is the Salt House." Ted pointed towards where the rocks and grass met on the far headland point, and where Bryn and Neets were probably still rummaging. "They make salt there from seawater but word has it the building is used for other, less legal purposes. If you look over to our right behind those trees you'll see the manor house. A family called Lewis lives there." Ted paused theatrically. "Wait a minute, wasn't that the name of the people you want to know about?" I nodded. "Well there we are then. We have the house, but where are the people I wonder? Could they be hiding? Could they even now be creeping up on you, because you won't leave them in peace?" The last words were said as though he was telling a children's spooky story. The only bits missing were the hands in the air and the stupid ghostly *Wooo, Wooo* noises.

I turned and stared at Ted. "That's a strange thing to say and an even stranger way of saying it." I dropped down from the wall and nervously brushed stone dust off my robes. "I have a sneaking suspicion there are things you're not telling me. What's more I'm probably not going to like hearing them."

The bald giant smiled at me without humour. "You don't recognise me do you? I met many of your friends years ago and have every reason to resent your presence in my village. Prove me wrong and tell me why you should live. You have … oh, let's say ten seconds." Ted started to count.

"Because I want to?" I said it with just the hint of a tremor in my voice as I edged away from the giant. It was time to take the initiative. "Let me guess. You're not the real vicar are you?" It was a wild guess, if a bloody obvious one, but I hoped it would be enough to stop the man for at least a second so I could work out an escape plan.

"Very good," said the fake vicar, all traces of a Welsh accent gone. He easily cut off my retreat. "You're right, of course, the real vicar is down in the church trussed up like a chicken. Oh, he's not hurt, well not much. However please think of me as your worst nightmare because you will not be using the stairs to go down, whereas I assure you I will."

I was slowly being backed into a corner of the tower where there was only the unpleasantly quick way down to the churchyard. "I've done nothing to you." I protested, but Ted shrugged his shoulders, grinned devilishly and continued to advance. "Or maybe I have?"

"Girl, I've been watching for you ever since I saw you in the cellar with the boy…"

Ah! and *Oh piddle!*

"…and I can't allow you to disrupt my life for a second time. I can't allow that for two reasons."

"Please tell me both reasons in the greatest of detail." I said it in a verbal rush playing for time, in fact the very time of my life. I looked round desperately for any means of escape. "Take as long as you want." Leaping around on Nelson's column was a walk in the park compared to trying to stay alive on this church tower.

"Very well. Firstly I've built up a very profitable enterprise in this little village and secondly, a long, long time ago you and your friends caused me considerable trouble."

"Not enough detail … Mr Black Knight Lewis," I mumbled to myself, guessing like crazy as the giant of a man advanced again picking up a handy piece of wood as he did so. "Tell me all about your little enterprise here and I'd be fascinated to learn how we met in the past though I suspect I already know. Moreover, I ought to point out that I'm a fully qualified wizard and could easily turn you into a rabbit," I looked around, "or at least I could if I had my blasted staff. Bother!"

Ted picked up his stick and swung it experimentally, testing it for balance and head-denting qualities. "Be quiet, silly girl. I wouldn't bother shouting for help either. You could scream up here and no one would ever take notice." To prove his point Ted bellowed at the top of his voice. "The interfering brat is up here, but soon she'll be down there!" He put his hand to his ear and pretended to listen intently. "No, not a peep. You see no one cares, so you'll just have to die alone and in silence."

My back pressed against the low wall and I began to think that the great days of Tertia the temporal detective and apprentice wizard could be over before they'd even started. Worse still, this was my first holiday in ages and it had to end so badly when it wasn't even raining. As a final humiliation, Ted took out the small lace handkerchief and offered it to me.

"Perhaps you'd like to wipe away a tear or two before you fly, or would you like to have a little blow? It's time to depart I'm afraid."

I took the piece of lace but decided it was probably too small to be effective as a parachute. I was at a loss for anything else to do, then read the monogrammed initials that confirmed at last I was right. I pointed at

Ted. "I know who you really are. **GP** is Guinevere Pendragon. You're that thieving, murdering bastard that almost toppled Camelot and nearly killed my parents. You're the Black Knight!"

"How astute and that's even more reason for you to die."

"But you had hair in Camelot, lots of it, and here as well. I saw you on your horse less than an hour ago and you were definitely hairy then, but now you're bald except for the beard."

"A minor accident in Camelot."

"But the man I saw come into the cellar had hair and no beard."

"A major wig. Time to fly, girl." He pulled off the false beard and cast it to one side. Evidently there wasn't much about the man you could trust.

"But you galloped away when I saw you in the lane."

"Not away, girl. I doubled back and followed you. When I realised where you were headed I dealt with the Reverend Lewis and waited for you."

"But why disguise yourself as the vicar and try to kill me?"

"It's partly because I love the theatrical side of life and let's face it, I'm the Black Knight with no name. However mostly it's because you're completely unknown here and your fall from the tower will be another tragic accident soon forgotten; you'll just disappear as will your little friends when they come to find you, because I will be waiting. And now prepare to die." He made a lunge for me and I tried to dodge to one side, but gorillas aren't easy to avoid.

I kicked, gouged, and scratched using every dirty trick I knew and stood back as the Black Knight gave a groan and slowly collapsed in a heap, clutching the growing lump on the back of his head. Inspector Smollett put the police truncheon back in his pocket, wiping his hands in satisfaction.

"I'm not really supposed to carry this thing anymore," he said almost apologetically, "but I like to for old time's sake. Just as well, as it's turned out."

I grinned and ran my fingers through my hair. "Mr Inspector, right now I think you're the most wonderful man in the world." I grabbed his head in both hands and gave him a massive and very noisy kiss on the forehead. "Come on, let's get down those stairs before you remember you hate heights, and baldy here wakes up."

Half way down the stairs Smollett not only remembered he couldn't stand heights, but that he also became a quivering wreck in confined spaces. He descended the remaining steps in seconds and erupted through the doorway into the church nave with a half-suppressed whimper. I followed at a more sedate pace and locked the door after me.

A sound like a cat with a sore throat reminded me we weren't alone. I ran to the rear of the church and cautiously peered round a screen just in case the Black

Knight had a noisy accomplice hiding there, but the figure in front of me was no threat and had definitely been the victim of a knot-and-gag expert with an excess of rope. The man was the absolute opposite of the unconscious impostor. He was short, thin, had a full head of dark, bushy hair, and was almost completely covered from head to toe in a bell-rope.

I grabbed Smollett by the arm and between us we managed to unravel the little man until he was almost recognisable as a vicar. The gag came off last which was just as well because some of his words were decidedly unvicarish and more navy bluish.

I waited patiently. "Finished?" The verbal flood died down and I got a reluctant nod. "Good. The nasty piece of work that did this to you is fast asleep at the top of your tower." I paused and cocked my head to one side. "However, knowing him he won't lie down for long and I may have locked the door, but if there's another way down he'll find it. Er ... is there?"

The vicar snorted. "Of course not, it's a church tower, not a public thoroughfare. There's only one way up and the same way down. Unless of course he uses the ivy and can climb like a monkey."

"More like a gorilla!" I said. "You mean he could climb down the outside of the tower all the way to the ground?"

"I suppose he could, but he'd need to be incredibly agile, extremely brave and very stupid." The vicar laughed. "Probably all three, so I would think he's safe up there."

"Rule out *stupid*," I said, "because he certainly isn't, but two out of three's not bad, which means he's probably already down and gone."

"Who's got away?" asked Smollett as he paced like a good copper. "I'd like to know who we're chasing, or more precisely who's been trying to kill us. Before I hit him over the head you told the gorilla you knew his name, but Black Knight is not a name, it's a colourful title. What aren't you telling me?" He stabbed the air with a stubby finger.

"I will, but not in front of the Rev." I gave the tiniest of nods towards the vicar who was concentrating on massaging circulation back into his bloodstream. "Don't fret, Mr Inspector. There are some things he really shouldn't know and the truth about the man who bopped him is probably one of them. Meanwhile why don't you go and check the tower and make sure the creep isn't escaping."

As I watched Smollett stomp out of the church I wondered why on earth Marlene had insisted he should come along. To save my life ... okay, that worked, but Marlene couldn't have foreseen him doing that, so there had to be some deep inner purpose as yet hidden from a dimwit like me. His sharp, incisive, analytical brain and devilishly clever insight? Do me a favour, I thought, and turned to the vicar.

"Your name isn't Ted by any chance, is it?"

"No," said the vicar, "whatever gave you that idea. My name's Frank. Frank Lewis. Not very Welsh I know, but I'm Frank by name and frank by nature." He rubbed his hands together to make sure I didn't miss his little joke. I gave a polite grin and then realised what he'd said.

"You're a Lewis? A real Lewis, like the sort that lives in the manor house?"

"Why, yes, we're not related though. It's amazing how many Lewises there are around here. I can trace my family back ... oh, let's see now, well a hundred years. Why?"

I put my arm round the reverend's shoulder. "Reverend ... can I call you that?" He nodded. "Thanks, Rev. You didn't see who clobbered you by any chance, did you?" He shook his head. "That's what I thought."

Smollett burst through the church door. Or at least he would have except the thing was so big, so heavy and its hinges so rusty that with all my inspector's strength it only creaked open a foot at a time, which made the finger flick by the Black Knight all that more impressive.

"He's escaped!" He paused for affect as he stumbled amongst the pews. "At least I think he has. Either way you're going to need some more ivy, Reverend, because the whole lot's come away from the tower, top to bottom and I reckon if he came down that way he had a bumpy landing and serves him bloody well right. Still, I reckon he's fled."

"Good," I said, much to Smollett's astonishment. "Well, we certainly don't want him hanging round here. I wouldn't know what to do with him for one thing, and he'll almost certainly go back from where he came now he's given us a warning. It may not have been the permanent one he was hoping for, but he'll believe it was effective."

"And was it?" asked Smollett.

"Not at all," I said with a grin. "Most bullies like him forget that people like us don't like threats. We won't hide in a little hole, we'll come up and smack 'im one. Come on, let's go and meet the others."

It was low tide and the beach was deserted with only three sandcastles for me to jump on, and as one looked just like a roughed-up Camelot I couldn't resist smashing it into a million grains of sand. Smollett tried to keep up with me, leaping from mound to mound and giggling in a most un-copper-like way, but there wasn't much left after I'd finished bouncing on the castles. The Salt House loomed ahead, looking like a pile of rubble surrounded by a number of random walls. It reminded me of a Camelot farmhouse after one of the Black Knight's raids, but without the dying screams and choking smoke.

Neets waved as she and Bryn walked towards us on the low coastal path surrounding the bay. We waited for them to join us because the Lewis mansion was going to be far more interesting than the Salt House, if only from the Time Portal point of view, and the mansion was on the other side of the village.

"Anything worth looking at, Neets?" I was pretty sure there wouldn't be.

"Not really. Bryn says the place has a couple of hidden cave rooms he remembers from when he was a kid and he's pretty sure one of them had two iron rings fastened to a wall. He says people reckon the wreckers round here tie people they don't like to the rings and watch them drown as the tide comes in."

"And if they really hate someone, Neets, they probably do it twice!"

We'd only been in 1734 for an hour or so and already I'd nearly been murdered, found out for certain the worst villain in Camelot was living here, and found out how the bad guys got rid of their enemies … and I had good reason to think I was one. Things were definitely looking up for the Agency.

It was time to go on the offensive and put our plan into effect, which only needed us to do one thing. We badly needed to think up a plan.

Chapter Four

Saints and Sinners

I could have sworn Neets and Bryn were holding hands as we walked back to the village, in Bryn's case full of nervousness and in Neets's case full of Bryn. Smollett planted himself in front of me in that official way police everywhere use to hold up the traffic.

"Before we try to find whatever it is we're looking for," he said when the others were safely out of earshot, "you promised you'd tell me who the gorilla was." My inspector had the air of a man who wasn't going to budge until he got what he wanted and right now he wanted an answer. Unfortunately for him I had the air of a girl who was fast disappearing up the beach desperately in search of a cup of tea. "Or possibly not, as the case may be," I heard him mutter as he followed me.

The village was deserted, except for a yapping dog that ran round our heels telling us to either keep away or throw a stick. All the people were presumably hiding in their homes having listened to a long sermon about fire and brimstone.

"Never mind tea," said Bryn when we reached the centre of the village. "If you're really desperate you can get a drink of water over there from the pump," he pointed to a horse trough with a tall spout and lever handle at its head. "And if you keep on about my dad being evil and the man who tried to kill you in the church I might have to give you a smack." Neets and Bryn sat on the side of the stone edge while I pumped the handle and slurped water, resisting the almost overpowering urge to pull the other two backwards and give them a good dunking. I did make sure the water I poured back into the trough splashed their necks wiping the silly smiles off their faces.

"Right then, so what's next?" I sat next to Bryn, kicking my heels against the stone. "I suppose you're going back to your place to keep an eye on your father, which leaves us two girls all alone in this strange village." I put a hand on his arm and gave him what was supposed to be a sweetly winning smile. "What's to become of us, I wonder?"

Bryn said nothing and Neets answered for him. "You're going back to school and I'm going to be a maid." I nearly fell into the trough as Bryn grinned, gave a grunt that to me was as good as saying *gotcha!* and walked back up the road leaving us to follow him in our own time.

"You what?" I laughed, but I had a feeling my laughter would be temporary. "School? Me? Don't talk such…"

59

Suddenly *tosh* was definitely not strong enough a word and I left it as an unsaid blank. "I don't believe it, you're serious!"

"It's not my idea," Neets protested, "and I don't particularly want to wash dishes and make beds for Bryn's father, but that's what Marlene told Bryn we have to do, so we will."

"But she isn't here." I wasn't going to take it lying down, or in any other position come to that. "Marlene can't know what's going on and deciding what we're going to do from three hundred years away is just her being bossy again. Anyway, back home I'm already sort of at college and I'm way too old to go back to school."

"Not as a teacher you're not." Neets managed to keep a straight face. "It's ironic really because you're going to teach the young kiddies how to read and write. There should be some interesting spelling results by the time you've finished. Bryn's arranging it all now."

I was only slightly annoyed. "And I'd like to see how many dishes survive after you've finished doing the washing up. Use 'em, smash 'em's always been your idea of housekeeping. I suppose it's the same with me and kids in a way. Should be interesting all round. Anyway, how can you be a maid in Bryn's house now his father knows we're here? Your cover's blown before you've even started."

Neets smiled and I knew Bryn had already thought of that. "Bryn says his father never goes into the servants' quarters so he'll never see me and he certainly won't expect you to be a teacher."

"You bet your life on that one! But I want to look around the house first, so I'm going to be maid number two for a few hours."

A cough from the shadow of a nearby house made us

all turn.

"There doesn't seem anything for me to do then." I'd almost forgotten my inspector in the shock of becoming a teacher. "Your witch partner back in the twenty-first century seems to have left me out of her plans, so if nobody minds I'm going to do some snooping around and see what I can dig up using good old modern policing methods." I suspected this might involve his truncheon again, but said nothing as he plodded out of the square in no particular direction.

Bryn took us into the mansion's scullery where amazingly the head housekeeper was expecting a new maid to start work just at that precise moment. I tried to explain that I was very temporary, like I'd be around for one day, and was actually the new school teacher, but she brushed aside my protests and insisted that a second permanent maid would be a nice bonus. Bryn had done his work well, the pig!

To say that Mrs Blodwyn Jones, our new boss, was on the large size would have been like saying Merlin was quite a good little conjuror, yet she immediately made us feel at home with a hot cup of tea and a slice of bread covered in beef dripping. With her rosy-cheeked complexion and healthy enthusiasm she was a country woman through and through and looked like everyone's favourite granny. Well … auntie, maybe. She also laughed a lot, seemingly out of genuine pleasure, which I found rather strange considering who the villainous master of the house was. Unless, of course, she was in the wrecking business and sank ships by jumping on them.

Neets's duties sounded simple enough and I thought very appropriate. Get up in the freezing cold before everyone else and make up fires in all the rooms, then prepare a morning cup of tea for all the other servants. Generally clean up throughout the day, making sure that all the washing and ironing is done on time, and then go to bed after everyone else once the fires have been damped down. She also had to do the dusting, which was about the only duty that could possibly put her face to face with Bryn's father. For all this she was to be paid the sum of one shilling a week, with free food and her own room. Considering this was one shilling more than Merlin or Marlene had ever paid I reckoned she was well in. I decided to give it a day, take the money, then become a teacher.

We saw nothing of Bryn, though Neets did hear he'd been locked in his room until he learned not to meddle in other people's business. Considering in Camelot the Black Knight's normal punishment for a first minor offence had been death I reckoned he'd got off bloody lightly. Besides, Bryn was *upstairs gentry* and we were *downstairs maids,* which said it all.

That evening after all the chores had been completed and the dinner plates washed and stacked (at least those that weren't smashed), Neets and I joined the others in the kitchen. Mrs Jones, young David (who showed no sign that he recognised us), and the rest of the servants were sitting around the great fire when I broke the silence. "Mrs Jones, please tell me about Mr Lewis. I've heard so much about the man, but I've never seen a glimpse of him. What's he like?"

The housekeeper sipped her tea and smiled at the new English maids. Neets had given up trying to put on a Welsh accent within minutes. "If you must know," she said, "and I'm not saying it's your place to know, he's a wonderful man, and there isn't a person in our village who will say a word against him."

Probably got them all scared witless, I thought.

"There are people round here who would have starved if it wasn't for the master," continued Mrs Jones, "and others who wouldn't have lived long enough to have even starved. The man's a saint and I'm proud to be able to serve him, as are we all."

This did not sound like a frightened woman, nor did she seem particularly witless. Therefore she was obviously either very deluded, or an excellent actress and I decided that nobody was that good without being on the stage.

"He's seriously that nice?" I half expected a *well he does eat babies for breakfast and murder people so he can relax at night as an alternative to a cup of hot milk, but other than that...* "I heard a rumour that he's a smuggler, wrecks boats on the cliffs, and kills the sailors if they reach the shore."

Mrs Jones moved so quickly that I thought she was going to smack me, but instead the housekeeper pushed herself forward so she was just inches from my face. She spoke very quietly, which made each word and syllable feel like a slap.

"Never, ever let me hear you say anything like that again." The words were hissed. "Don't even think it. Your job is to serve and clear up here, not to pass judgment on people better than you'll ever be." Mrs Jones eased herself back into her seat and gradually her face relaxed into a smile. "I'm sorry, dear, I'm sure you didn't mean what you said, but round here Mr Lewis is looked upon as a saint. And you don't criticise a saint." She threw her head back and roared with laughter.

"I'm sorry, Mrs Jones," I said with what I hoped was suitable humbleness. "I wasn't thinking. Please excuse me."

The atmosphere in the kitchens relaxed and the other servants returned to their own small conversations, soon forgetting the rude little foreign girl's sideshow.

"No problem, dear. I'll put it down to the fact you're English. Now it's getting late, so you run along and do your chores. Take Unita with you." She nodded towards my cousin sitting quietly in the corner. "You'll have everything done twice as quickly then."

Neets and I made a beeline for the rear stairs and ran up them to the first floor bedrooms. I was genuinely shocked by what had just happened in the kitchen. On one hand we knew that the Black Knight was an evil thug capable of murder and yet everyone seemed to think Bryn's father was simply wonderful. It was all wrong. I opened the biggest, most ornate door, peeped in and knew at once I'd chosen the right one. "I want to turn down the bedclothes in Mr Lewis's room while he's out and while we're doing it see what we can find out about him. Something doesn't add up." I entered the room, making sure the place was deserted, and beckoned Neets to follow.

"This is a man's room," she said looking at the furnishings. "There's not a sign of a woman's touch anywhere."

"A woman? Like who?"

"Like his wife."

"I didn't know Mr Lewis was married? Nobody's mentioned a wife." I turned down the bedclothes, took the warming pan from its rest near the fire and slipped it between the sheets. "Besides, the thought of any woman falling in love with the Black Knight seems pretty incredible."

"Bryn told me she died soon after he was born," Neets said, leaving me to do the work as usual, "and for months

64

his father wouldn't leave the house. He went into a shell, refused to talk to anyone and either brooded in his room or wandered aimlessly round the gardens. Everyone was very worried about him, but even more about Bryn. A boy needs a dad."

"So, what happened?" I'd started to rummage through the chest of drawers, looking for anything incriminating and making sure I put things back where I found them like any good detective.

"The strangest thing!" said Neets, letting me do the rummaging. "Everyone says that for a year or so this was a pretty lawless place before Bryn's father came here. People didn't dare go out at night, violence was rampant and the village had a terrible reputation for smuggling and wrecking ships to steal their cargo. This was not the sort of place people moved to out of choice, and those who lived here couldn't move away. Then Mr Lewis arrived."

"Ah, the Black Knight. So he took over and it all got worse?"

"Apparently not," said Neets. "He organised the village into a sort of local militia force, and made sure that if anyone was attacked, or was even threatened, they got justice. He was even made the local magistrate. And then Bryn's mum died."

"And he started to brood?" I was still searching through the drawers.

"Yes. And all the old villainy came back with a vengeance, far worse than before really, so that violence and even murders became common. The master, I mean Bryn's dad, started to go out every night with his riders like he used to and things went downhill from there."

This time I did look up. "He still rides out every night with his men?"

"Yes, and Bryn said he comes back the next morning looking dog tired. More often than not he's soaking wet and covered in cuts and bruises."

"He's not nipping down to the pub for a quick pint then." I'd drawn a blank in the chest of drawers. "So where do you reckon he goes, Neets?" I closed the last drawer and moved over to the wardrobe opposite the window.

"No idea. Out wrecking? But then Bryn says the villagers think he and his men are, wonderful."

I carried on looking through the wardrobe and was beginning to think that Mrs Jones might have been right after all about Mr Lewis being a saint. Then I found what I'd been looking for. "Got it!" I grabbed a bundle of clothes from the bottom of the wardrobe and threw them on the bed.

"Got what?" Neets stared at the clothes. "It's just a lot of old rags."

"Old clothes that look very familiar," I said in triumph. I arranged the trousers, shirt, jerkin, hat and assorted accessories into the shape of a man and stood back looking thoughtful. "I've seen these before and not so long ago either."

"What do you mean?" Neets could be quite dense at times. "They're just clothes. There's nothing wrong with them."

"Only two things. They're not from anywhere round here and they're not even from this century. This is the sort of stuff people used to wear in Camelot about a thousand years ago."

"That's clever, Tersh. And what's the clincher, because there usually is one?"

She was right, of course. "The clincher is this." I pulled out a bundle from the rear of the wardrobe about the size of a football. With the flourish of a magician (or wizard if I'm going to be picky) I took off the rags and threw the Black Knight's helmet on the bed. "There's no doubt now, Neets. Whatever anybody says about him, Bryn's father is our old enemy. He's behind everything from smuggling and shipwrecking to the disappearance of Marble Arch and the replacement of Nelson's statue with the far from statuesque me. Case mostly solved. All we need now is to catch him red-handed and find out why."

The problem was I had no idea what we were going to do next, except maybe get my Inspector Smollett to arrest him with his truncheon. I almost laughed.

I looked out the window. The moon had just disappeared behind a cloud and there was the definite threat of a storm on the horizon. This was perfect wrecking weather and we now knew not only who was leading the wreckers, but we had proof of his real identity.

We had to do something, and soon before the Black Knight came after us.

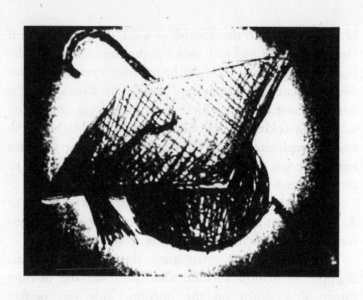

Chapter Five

Teachers and Wreckers

The next day I sort of gave my notice by sneaking out of the back door and wandering down to the village to take up my true vocation as a teacher. The only person who saw me go was the ever-present David, who said nothing and gave me a smiley wave.

The village school was a small building with classrooms either side of an entrance hall where coats and bags could be left. Above the door was a small sign *Port Eynon Junior Skool. Est. 1718.* Two things struck me. Firstly, the school was only sixteen years old, and secondly whoever made the sign couldn't spell. I was in good company.

Bryn had told me the head teacher was a dragon feared by every child in the area, but I decided it couldn't be worse than facing up to the Black Knight and his murderous thugs when they raided my parents' farm back in Camelot, so I flipped a mental coin, took a deep breath, and opened the door to the classroom on the left.

The room was packed and all conversation stopped as every face turned in my direction. I smiled bravely and gave a small self-conscious wave. Some of the children waved back ... girls not boys, I noticed.

"Hi, everybody, I'm the new teacher," I said cheerfully. I decided that *cheerfully* might just win everybody over. "My name's Tertia and I'm here to ... er, teach you. Well maybe not all of you. That is to say maybe none of you. Just those that the drag ... sorry, the head teacher tells me to teach." My brow was beginning to sweat and I wondered briefly if Mrs Jones would take me back as a downstairs maid. This teaching business was tough.

The woman sitting behind a large desk at the front of the room stood up, stared at me for several painfully stern seconds before lighting up the room with the most radiant smile I'd ever seen. She beckoned me forward.

"Welcome, my dear," she said, greeting me like an equal. "I was told we could expect you, but I must admit I was expecting another old dragon like myself, not someone actually nearer the children's age than mine. Children, say hallo to Miss Tertia. I think that is your name?"

The whole class stood up and bowed. Most of the kids were grinning broadly and not one looked in the slightest bit scared of the dragon. I began to wonder just how many days of school Bryn had actually skipped and how many he'd attended. I began to wonder whether he'd even met the head teacher, whose name I discovered was Miss Jones. Another odd coincidence.

"Boys and girls," Miss Jones said in that lecturing voice used by all teachers, "I want you to read the second chapter of our new book while I talk to Miss Tertia for ten minutes. Remember, silence, because I *will* be able to hear you."

In the small garden Miss Jones sat on a rustic bench, looked at the view over the village towards the bay, and smiled. She motioned to me and patted the seat. "Sit down, dear, and tell me about yourself as I want to know everything; where you come from, where you've taught before, and what your specialty is. Don't be shy. Then I'll tell you about myself."

I was tempted to suggest Miss Jones should go first because frankly I couldn't answer a single one of her questions without looking stupid and a liar. I reckoned I could get away with being one, but not both. I took a deep breath.

"I'm not from round here," I said, "I'm from a place called…"

"Yes, England I know. Don't worry, the children are fairly broad-minded."

"Ah, good," I said with a great deal of relief because saying I was from Camelot could have caused problems, "but I'm afraid I haven't done much teaching, at least not what you might call the basic subjects." It was probably not the time to mention wizardry and a possible ability to turn people into rabbits as my only qualifications.

Miss Jones tapped me on the arm. "In this day and age it's good to find any teacher, never mind someone who specialises. The important thing is to teach the children what you know."

Good idea, I thought, that's the morning taken care of.

"I always find a nature walk is good after lunch." It was as though Miss Jones had been reading my mind. "They love walking around the cliffs and on a nice day you couldn't ask for a more beautiful place to go for a stroll."

For November the day was relaxingly warm and I was beginning to feel I might actually like this teaching business as Miss Jones continued talking as though what she said wasn't really important, until…

"Was Camelot as nice as my village?" She waited for my reaction.

"Oh, tish!" I said after a pause and a gasp. "How

71

did you know? I mean I didn't let on and I didn't drop any clues, so who told you?"

Miss Jones shrugged. "I rather think I'd have guessed you weren't a real teacher given a couple of minutes, but you're right, I was told by Bryn."

"But he said you were an old dragon."

"Yes, but did he tell you I'm also his aunt?"

"You're kidding!" I nearly shouted. "No, he bloody well didn't. He's going to pay for this." I jumped up and hit my left palm with my right fist.

Miss Jones laughed. "I don't doubt it, but he felt you'd be safer working undercover with me. You are after all a detective, I believe?"

"Yes, er ... sort of."

"Well then, where better to hide your identity than with me where I can protect and help you."

I considered my options, which largely consisted of staying in the school with Miss Jones and using its cover to poke around the village ... or the other option, which was to do the opposite. I wasn't exactly sure what that was, so I decided on the school.

"Since you put it so nicely, I'll stay. But on one condition, that I get to hit Bryn next time I see him." I sat down again.

Miss Jones took my hand. "It's a deal. Now let me tell you a little bit more about myself because it's only fair now that I know about you. For a start, being Bryn's aunt, I was also his mother's sister. I lived with Marie and Blodwyn, our other sister, just outside

Swansea and when Marie was visiting friends near here she met Mr Lewis." Pretty soon I knew everything that Neets had already learned from Bryn, but with a bit more detail.

I sat on the bench swinging my legs, trying to think of something to say. *Oh!* just didn't seem enough, and *Wow, stupid bloody woman. Fancy going riding on a night like that!* was probably inappropriate. "Bryn never told me," I responded at last. "It *was* a long time ago though."

"Sixteen years. Yes, it's a long time, Tertia," replied Miss Jones, "but we all still remember that night. Blodwyn and I weren't here, we were at home in Swansea, but we came out the next day to help search and we moved here soon afterwards and Mr Lewis established the school for me. You see nobody has ever explained what really happened and why Marie's horse bolted the way it did is a mystery. She was a good horsewoman and her mare was well trained. Even after all this time I still hope to find out the truth and who knows, as a detective you might be able to help."

I had the grace to blush and Miss Jones had the grace not to notice as she led the way back into the school building.

"Come on, Miss Tertia, it's time for you to get started with your teaching duties. I'll take the class on the left and you take the one on the right and may the best woman win!"

For two days I enjoyed myself immensely. The children were polite enough, but at the start it was the total silence that got to me. The kids sat behind their desks and stared at me as I walked round the room. A cough, a blink, even a belch would have broken the ice, so I decided to talk about geography and history … Tertia style.

"I've been to a few places thousands of miles away," I said without exaggeration, "and seen things that would make your toes curl. Anyone interested in hearing about them?"

There were some low-level mumblings and a few shrugged shoulders before a boy at the back called out, "I been almost twenty miles to Swansea once and nearly got to Cardiff, Miss, but we didn't go in the end. You been as far as Swansea then, Miss? Have you? 'cos I've been farther than anyone!" he said proudly. I also felt it as a challenge.

"He has, Miss," said his friends.

"So where have you been then, Miss?" the boy was daring me to better him and this was put-up or shut-up time.

"Firstly, do you all believe in time travel?" I decided to get the tricky stuff out of the way early on and for the next hour told them about the beautiful Merlin and the handsome, but a bit thick Arthur, as well as the real story of Camelot. I told them about the royal sword Excalibur, the Knights of the Round Table – the good ones anyway – and some of our adventures.

As the minutes went by, both the children and I became more and more involved in the story as I started darting round the room acting out the scenes, while the kids sat there open mouthed and cheered when things got really exciting. Nobody except me noticed the door quietly open or saw Miss Jones enter the room and take a spare seat at the very rear of the class. Even I ignored her and carried on a mock sword fight with the boy who went to Swansea.

"...and so Merlin and Arthur went to live on Avalon while the rest of us joined up with her sister Marlene and became detectives." I looked round triumphantly. "Now who doesn't believe in time travel?"

A hand attached to an arm that was slightly longer than anyone else's went up at the back. "I must admit I'm becoming convinced," said Miss Jones, "your adventures sound absolutely fascinating."

The colour drained from my face because I hadn't meant to go this far. "They're only stories," I said hoping Miss Jones would understand.

"I know, dear," the head teacher replied, evidently enjoying herself, "but please go on. They're excellent."

With slightly less enthusiasm I spent the next hour reliving some of my more believable adventures back in Camelot with Neets, while the class cheered, applauded and some of the more excitable ones banged their desktops to show their appreciation. Miss Jones walked to the front of the class beaming happily and raised her arms for quiet.

"That," she said with emphasis, "was one of the best history lessons I have ever listened to. I could almost feel myself being in Sherwood Forest and I wanted to duck when the soldiers fired their arrows, it was so real. But no more today, children."

There was a disappointed chorus of "Oh, Miss!" and a solitary groan from the boy who'd been to Swansea.

"No, I'm sorry, but it's time to go home. Miss Tertia has taken up the entire afternoon with her wonderful history lesson. So now we'll say a short prayer, bid each other *good afternoon* and see you all tomorrow."

The children stood in silence with their heads bowed for a respectable thirty seconds, then marched into the garden where they became screaming kids again.

Miss Jones walked back from the window where she'd been watching the children playing in the road that led to the village centre. She looked at me and cocked her head to one side. She even put her hands on her hips, which made her look scarily like Merlin, but at least she wasn't tapping her foot, which would have been a very bad sign.

"A history story?" Miss Jones sat in the teacher's chair and smiled. "I'd love to think so, Tertia, I really would, but my instincts tell me you actually experienced what you just described. You were there,

76

weren't you?"

"Er, yes." I knew better than to deny it. I was standing in front of Miss Jones with hands clasped behind my back and eyes downcast like a naughty kiddy. Some detective, me!

"And you rescued Maid Marion?"

"Er, yes I did." I shuffled my feet.

"And made the Sheriff of Nottingham look silly?"

"Oh, no," I said. "Neets did that, but he didn't require much help from us."

"Ah, you mean Unita, your cousin from Camelot. Bryn told me about her as well. In fact he spoke rather a lot about her."

"He's got a big mouth has that nephew of yours." I punched my right fist into my left hand for the second time that day and winced because it hurt. "He's going to get a good smacking when I see him." I meant it, too.

"I don't doubt it," said Miss Jones, "and meanwhile we both know a lot more about each other than we did earlier today and that can only be good. For instance, if what Bryn told me is correct you're older than me by some thousand years. Which just goes to show that age does *not* bring wisdom, only wrinkles."

"I do *not* have wrinkles," I said, rubbing my face defiantly.

"Fair enough," said Miss Jones, "neither wrinkles, nor wisdom then." Before I could think of a reply she continued. "Tonight you're staying with me. I have a nice little cottage near the shore. You'll have your own room and total privacy, which most children round here don't have." She stood up as she spoke, checked the window locks, picked up her books and motioned me to leave the room so she could lock the door. "I'll cook tonight if you do the washing up and then tomorrow we'll swap over. Do we have a bargain?"

I nodded happily. This was home away from home, with the exception that for once when I told a story I had an audience that hung onto my every word and didn't accuse me of lying.

For two days I was as happy as a Camelot pig rolling in whatever it is pigs like to roll in and if I'd been given the option I would have quite honestly stayed as a teacher with Miss Jones. The trouble was I very quickly ran out of history stories and was beginning to repeat myself, not that the kids seemed to mind. Day three was beginning to look decidedly ominous so on the second night when Neets banged on the front door of Miss Jones's cottage and dragged me outside into the pouring rain, I wasn't too disappointed. Just very wet.

"What's up, Neets?" I said between gasps as we ran down a street that was fast becoming a river. We dodged the deeper puddles without much success and splashed our way to the shore.

"Wreckers, Tersh," Neets shouted over the noise of wind and lashing rain. "Bryn says the wreckers will be out tonight and we both know who'll be leading them."

I stopped running and looked at my cousin in amazement. "The wreckers are out wrecking ships and you reckon the two of us are going to stop them, as well as grab their leader?" I hid from the rain in a handy doorway. "Cool, kid, I like it!" I was getting back to my normal impetuous self. Being a teacher was fine, but a bit restricting after the first forty-eight hours.

As we passed by the Salt House we saw a dull light shining through one of the sea-stained windows. There was no movement, just the light, and neither of us was inclined to explore inside, especially after what Bryn had told us. Fighting murderous black knights was one thing, but eerie ghost-lanterns could be left until daylight. We walked up the path leading to the headland, which was mostly obscured by the rain, and the salt spray being whipped up by the wind flew like creamy froth into our faces.

"They'll be high up on the headland," Neets shouted above the noise of the growing storm as she grabbed me by the arm and led the way. The path branched off to the right, rising steeply towards the cliff top nearly a hundred threatening feet above us. The early rain had made the path slippery enough, but now there was a stream of water gushing down making progress difficult for anyone going up and a theme park ride for anyone stupid enough to want to go down. We were soon covered in mud and our clothes were torn by the brambles on either side of the path, but neither of us would have suggested going back. This was fun.

It took more than half an hour to climb what would have taken ten minutes on a normal day and when we reached the point where the path levelled off to become headland we collapsed in a sodden, gasping heap of limbs. I rolled over and looked at my grinning cousin. "It's good to be back, Neets," I shouted. "For a moment we were in danger of becoming sad old hags back there."

"Not to mention sensible. Now we're back to being…"

"Merl's Girls!" we chorused and laughed against the wind.

Being a Merl's Girl meant so many things. Like being an apprentice to the greatest wizard ever. Like being a time traveller. Like battling against some of the worst villains in history, mostly in the process of rescuing some pet or other. And now most important of all it meant being together on an adventure.

"Help!" The cry came from the rain-washed path and sounded urgent. "I'm slipping!" It was desperate. "I can't hold on much longer."

Neets crawled over to the cliff top and peered through the rain at the figure clinging precariously to a bramble root just below her. "Bryn, is that you?" It struck me as a silly question, because nobody would be stupid enough to be out on a night like this, except us of course. "Hang on. Grab this." Neets unwound her woollen belt and dangled it as near as she could to the stranded boy. Bryn grabbed it with one hand and carefully pulled himself up an inch at a time until he sprawled on the cliff top.

I looked at the boy lying at my feet and decided he was probably in the right place. "Bloody hell," I shouted over the wind, "what the hell are you doing here? Come on, get up. We haven't got time to waste on looking after you."

Bryn looked up and gratefully took Neets's hand as he got himself into a kneeling position and then stood, reeling slightly against the wind buffeting the headland. "Thanks," he muttered not really wanting to say it, especially to me, but I knew he meant it anyway. "Did you really both think you could go off without me? I brought you here you know and as I'm a man it's up to me to look after you and see you come to no harm."

Neets and I exchanged exasperated glances and Bryn had the sense to shut up as the three of us leaned into the wind and set off along the headland in search of wreckers.

Neets was right. Tonight was perfect for luring unsuspecting ships onto the rocks. What little moon there should have been was completely hidden by the thick, black clouds and even the clouds were obscured by the lashing rain driven in by the winds. Any ship would be grateful for the beacons strategically placed on the headland to show a safe passage and even though all sea captains knew the wreckers' beacons were probably alight as well, it was impossible to tell the difference on a stormy night. Bryn said a good captain had to use his best judgment and sometimes toss a coin.

I took a crafty glance at the lad and decided he might be a bit of a bozo, but deep down on the surface he really wasn't all that bad looking for a boy. If he played his cards right he stood a chance of a date, I reckoned, even if I was a thousand years older than him. Maybe he liked older women.

For what felt like an hour, but in reality was more like twenty minutes, we forced our way through the gale and drenching rain, looking out for the sheer cliff edge and any sign of the wreckers. Over a hundred feet below us the sea crashed on the rocks throwing spray high into the air, spelling doom for any stray ships. I grabbed Neets's arm and pointed into the darkness ahead of us, because even through the lashing storm I could make out a dim but definite light some way off. It was brighter than an ordinary lantern and as far as we could tell it was stationary.

"A beacon?" I grabbed Bryn's shoulder and pointed.

"There's no safety beacons on this stretch of coast," he said, "It's too dangerous. If it's a beacon then the wreckers lit it."

"Then we'd better put it out." Neets was getting into the spirit of things.

"Hang on," I shouted at the top of my lungs, "where there's a wrecker's beacon, there'll be wreckers. Big guys with nasty minds and probably guns and things."

"So?"

"Just thought I'd mention it. Let's go and put the bloody thing out!" I started running, or rather stumbling towards the light followed closely by Neets who was followed by an increasingly protective Bryn.

Up close the flaming beacon lit an area of at least twenty feet around the metal brazier and would have been visible far out to sea. We stayed outside the circle of light, looking for any sign that the wreckers might still be nearby, but saw nobody. Somehow I'd expected a group of obvious thugs to be there, staring into the darkness and searching for signs of an approaching victim, but maybe wreckers aren't so stupid, I decided. Either that, or the Black Knight's son was wrong about this bit of coast.

Bryn ran up to the brazier and using an old branch that presumably should have been fuel for the beacon, tried to topple it. "Help me," he grunted as he heaved on the branch, using it as a lever. "It's beginning to move."

I grabbed another branch to add my weight to Bryn's and by rocking the beacon backwards and forwards we built up enough momentum so that with a screaming of bending metal and the roaring crash of fire the brazier rolled onto its side spilling burning wood and hissing coals onto the soaked ground. Soon all that was left was steaming embers, scorched earth, and a descending darkness that seemed even more solid after the brilliant light of the beacon.

"We've done it, Neets," I shouted. "We've beaten the wreckers and more important, we've beaten their leader yet again. So much for the Black Knight!"

While we were congratulating ourselves Bryn was concentrating on the tall figure sitting silently on a stallion. It hadn't been there a moment earlier but now it seemed to loom over us. Slowly the horse trotted forward and I saw the man was holding a cocked pistol with a look of nonchalant menace. He stopped close to the dying embers.

Neets and I stared at the rider, knowing we had at last met up with the leader of the wreckers and a man who would want revenge not only for tonight, but for what we did to him in Camelot. We looked closer.

"You!" I cried in astonishment as the rider took off his hat so I could see his features for the first time.

The man swore, stared first at Neets, then at me and burst out laughing as he walked his horse slowly towards us. He took out a second pistol and I knew that our adventure was about to take a turn.

Chapter Six

Old Friends and New Spies

"We meet again," said the rider and I remembered the last time he'd spoken to us had been in Camelot, "though I must admit I didn't expect it would be more than a thousand years in the future and in another country." We gaped in silence. "Do you have nothing to say to an old friend?" He dismounted, walked over and gave each of us a welcoming hug. He passed his two pistols to Bryn and told him to keep the powder dry.

Eventually my brain remembered to close my

mouth to something approaching normal, which still meant it was open. "Sir Gawain," I said with a gasp, "it can't be you. The White Knight. We never guessed."

"We reckoned you were the Black Knight," said Neets. "I mean, the wrecking, the murders, the clothes we found in your house. Everything pointed to you being the Black Knight." She looked dismayed and took a defensive step back from our old friend. "Does this mean you're behind it all? Are you responsible for all the deaths and wrecking?"

"You can't be," I said. "You're good, and I mean we helped you back in Camelot. You're..." I searched for the right word, "...charismatic. You're the White Knight."

Sir Gawain smiled. "Don't worry, in spite of what you might have heard I'm still the good guy." He peered through the streaming rain along the headland stretching either side of us. "If the wreckers are operating tonight it's not round here so we might as well pack in and go home. You both look as though you could do with a change of clothes and some warmth." He turned to Bryn. "And that goes for you too, my son. You'll find spare horses over there." He pointed to a spot a hundred yards away where a small group of men waited patiently. He called to them, his voice carrying over the noise of the wind. "Bring three of the best mounts over here. Bryn will help select them." I suspected they had been waiting for the command, but it was impressive and so like the Gawain of old.

Neets watched Bryn walk away. "He's a Gawain? My Bryn's your son?" she said, not bothering to hide her surprise, or the *my* come to that.

"Of course he's my son, but as far as Bryn's concerned his name is Lewis and so is mine. Please remember that. I'll explain everything when we get back to the house."

"This beacon we tipped over," I said pointing at the still smoking embers, "wasn't that a wrecker's signal?"

"It was, but not intended for ships to see," said Gawain. "It was a false one intended to bring me here. The wreckers wanted us far away from their real beacons which I suspect are farther down the coast near Rhossili, so they set up false beacons and got one of their people to quietly spread the word that it'll be lit. I had no choice but to come here. One day I'll catch them and stop their murderous activities. That'll also be the day I avenge myself on the Black Knight for what he did to me and my family."

Before we could ask him any more questions Bryn returned with the horses, one of which I presumed was obviously his own from the way it nuzzled his cheek when he caressed its ears. Neets selected a beautiful piebald leaving me with the reddest, smallest and calmest horse I'd ever seen. It was a donkey and for some reason I couldn't comprehend I reckoned I'd got the best of the bunch. Gawain remounted his stallion, and we got on our horses with varying degrees of skill.

"I'll explain more when we get home…" he looked at Bryn, "to all of you, I promise." Gawain spurred his horse into a trot and the three of us followed close behind intent on not getting lost in the rain-sodden darkness.

Neither Neets nor I had been within several feet of a horse in ages, and bloody horses have a knack of knowing when a rider is out of practice. The mounts Bryn selected for us played *'Whoops, nearly went over the cliff then'* and *'Sorry about the thorn bush and the low hanging branch'* plus *'Honest, I didn't see the rabbit scrape I tripped over'*, and their favourite, *'Look at me, I can stand on my two back legs and paw the air'*. I vowed to give my donkey a good talking to when we got back to Bryn's house. Yes, I had a donkey, much to Neets's amusement.

Once the horses and donkey were safely stabled and scolded (though I did tickle my donkey's ears so he'd know I didn't really mean it), we all made our way into the large manor house and were welcomed by Mrs Jones as though she hadn't seen us for a month. She found a change of clothes for everyone, sat us down in Gawain's study and fussed around until she was sure we had food, drink, and warmth from the roaring log fire.

The study was more a room where Gawain could

relax and not be interrupted than a private library for contemplation. There were bookshelves, though most of them were stacked with novels intended to entertain rather than educate and the central point of the room was the large hearth rather than a desk. None of us felt we were invading his privacy, but that we were welcome guests.

Gawain looked at Neets and me and smiled with sincere pleasure, even though his carefully constructed cover had been blown. He was now going to have to explain to us what he was doing in Port Eynon, but more importantly he needed to break it gently to Bryn that his father was not who he thought and was actually from the previous millennium and a Camelot knight to boot!

"It's good to see both of you again, it really is," said Gawain, as he carefully pushed a smouldering log further into the fire, sending sparks high into the chimney and giving the room a cheery Christmas warmth, "and before you ask me what I'm doing here I'm going to ask you the same question." He laughed. "After all I am the magistrate and Lord of the Manor as Bryn will tell you and as such I have more right to be here than you do. Let's face it, it can't be a coincidence we all meet up miles and years from anywhere." He crossed his arms and smiled with the charisma we remembered so well.

I broke first. "We're chasing a load of weird coincidences dressed up as purple herrings…"

"Red," whispered Neets. "You mean red coincidences and soused herrings."

"…and that's about it," I continued, ignoring my cousin's interruption. "We're not really sure what's going on except that I've been dragged round loads of places in time and seem to have picked up some pretty undesirable things, like your Bryn for one, not that he's all that undesirable, and a weird statue of some sailor Lord or other."

"Statue?" Gawain showed more than polite interest.

"Yeh, I took its place on this great big column thing, and I tell you it was bloody cold up there."

"Statue?" Gawain repeated the word as though the rest of my explanation counted for nothing. He prodded the fire again absentmindedly. "Tell me what it looked like and where it is now." He stared into the flames.

"It's in Merlin's cave if you must know." I was annoyed that Gawain should consider a statue more important than me. "It looked like a tall bloke with an arm missing and a patch over one eye. Oh, and he had a weird hat."

"Excellent," said Gawain, "and you say his eye patch is still in place and the rest of him is intact."

"Yeh, he's got three limbs and one eye if you reckon that makes him intact. He's also taking up far too much room in Galahad's restaurant."

"My apologies to my old friend Galahad," said Gawain. "You do mean *the* Sir Galahad, the one who found the Holy Grail?"

"No, the one who founded the *Olé Grill* restaurant chain," I said with a little huff. "Blimey! Everyone wants him to be some sort of romantic hero and all he wants to be is a famous restaurant owner."

My memories of Camelot were mainly of rain, mud, cold, wind (mostly because of the food), leaky buildings, and smells. How on earth people got this idea of knights in shining armour rescuing maidens, killing dragons, and finding Holy Grails all over the place completely beats me. All the knights I knew were either fat, extremely old, half mad, or reinventing themselves as business men of one sort or another.

"Very well, I suppose I'd better explain how and why I'm here."

"Now there's a thought," I mumbled.

"I came here after the Black Knight," said Gawain. "You remember him? He tried to overthrow Arthur and laid waste to half of Camelot."

"We remember," said Neets, "and we've already come up against him here, or at least Tersh has."

I gazed at Gawain and saw the familiar trustworthy features. "And now you've set us a puzzle because we not only know the Black Knight and what he's like, but we had you nailed as being him, or rather him being you. Everything pointed to it. The wrecking, smuggling, murders, and some of what Bryn said sort of wrapped it up. So both you and the Black Knight are here?"

"Oh yes, he's here and he hasn't changed. He arrived about a year before me and lost no time in terrorising the area with a new gang of thugs. I've done what I can to stop him, but he has spies everywhere. He knows what I'm planning almost before I do and all I've really managed is to slow him down a bit." Gawain paused. "In return for which he killed my wife Marie and deprived Bryn of his mother."

"How did you both get here?" I beat Neets to the question by a microsecond. "We all saw your armies fighting outside the walls of Camelot and you defeated the Black Knight in single combat. The classic White Knight versus the Black Knight fight. You brought him into the castle. We all saw you. So how come he wasn't strung up like he deserved?"

"Between the castle gates and the dungeons my men were attacked and the Black Knight was set free. I told you he had powerful friends, but even I didn't think they'd attack inside Camelot itself."

"But we all know he was executed. We saw it happen." I was puzzled.

"We couldn't afford to let anyone know he escaped and was still alive, so another condemned traitor agreed to dress up as the Black Knight and take his place."

"What? Just like that?" said Neets. "The man volunteered and you didn't break his fingers first?"

"Certainly not! We're not animals," said Gawain. "Normally the condemned man's estates would be confiscated leaving his family homeless, but I promised him his wife and children would keep their home and be given a pension for life. Furthermore, I made sure his death was quick and he suffered as little as possible."

"That must have been a great consolation," I said with a hint of sarcasm.

"He was a multiple murderer," said Gawain. "He knew what his fate was going to be and he considered himself fortunate."

"So what happened to the Black Knight?"

"I traced him to his hiding place in Camelot and nearly captured him. We fought and he was so good I thought I'd met my match, but eventually I began to get the better of him, and as I was about to beat the man he jumped out of a window and disappeared into the alleyways. The strangest thing, though, I grabbed his hair as he jumped and the whole lot came away in my hand. The man was completely bald!"

"We know," I said. "We've seen him here twice."

"So he escaped again," said Neets with a tut. "Typical."

"Typical of him, or typical of me?" said Gawain with what sounded like genuine interest.

"Typical of a man!" said Neets, though for the life of me I couldn't think why she said it. It was most unlike her and far more like something Marlene would come out with after a couple of whiskeys on a Friday night.

"Well, at least I'm a man then," said Gawain with a laugh, "and you, Unita, are no longer a girl. You've become a beautiful young woman who would make any handsome lad proud to have her on his arm, and I'm including my son in that." He nodded towards Bryn who was busy sorting papers and possibly just out of earshot.

"You're kidding?" Neets said with a gasp and a blush.

"You're kidding!" I gagged *very* quietly. There's never a sick-bag lying around when you want one.

"Over the next few days," continued Gawain, "rumours came from all over Camelot as to where the Black Knight had gone to, most of which I could discount, but one was worth investigating. One of my informants claimed to have seen him going into the workshop apartments Merlin used to have in one of the castle's towers. I checked and sure enough he was there, but instead of fighting me he laughed, jumped through a shimmering ultraviolet archway, and disappeared."

"It must have been one of Merlin's experimental Time Portals!" I said. "And you followed him immediately?"

"No. I had no idea what had happened. I just knew he was no longer there and I could have been following him to certain death. I asked Merlin to explain about the archway and she – yes, I know her little secret – agreed to send me to wherever the Black Knight had gone, although she couldn't guarantee the time would be accurate."

"So you arrived a year too late?"

"Yes."

"But how come you and the Black Knight both ended up with Portals?" A bloody good question by Neets for a change and I wished I'd thought of it first.

"The Portal Merlin was experimenting with was her first portable one and the Black Knight took it with him. Merlin knew that and allowed me to take one as well. As she said, it was only fair. Not only was it portable, it could also transport things remotely," he looked at me, "like you and a certain statue."

I looked at Gawain as he played with the pommel of his sword and stared into the fire. "So what happened when you got here?"

"The Black Knight, his name here is Schwartz by the way just as mine is Lewis, had set up his wrecking and terrorism gang about a year before I arrived and it took some time before people accepted me as a local and a friend. Meanwhile Schwartz went from strength to strength and there was little I could do about it. Then two years after I met and married Marie, Bryn was born and my beautiful wife was killed by Schwartz. His murderous wrecking and smuggling got worse and I was a defeated man.

"But I thought you ran the smuggling," I said.

"Up to a point, certainly what you might call the legitimate smuggling that benefits the local community, but Schwartz runs everything else and has a small army protecting him."

"Gawain," I said, risking my big mouth again, "can I ask how Bryn's mum died. Nobody's ever really said."

"I believe Marie was killed by Schwartz as a warning that I should stop interfering in his activities. His men ambushed her one night as she was riding her horse back home from visiting friends and scared it so badly it bolted over the cliffs into the sea. We never found any trace of her, or the horse. Any witnesses were bribed into silence by Schwartz, but one or two people who know me well told me what happened and I—" He stopped suddenly and turned round. "Bryn!"

While his father had been talking, Bryn had walked quietly up behind him and now stood face to face with a man who must have seemed a stranger to him.

"Bryn, I didn't want you to hear it this way," said Gawain. "I've wanted to tell you ever since your mother died, but it was never the right time and I was afraid you might take the law into your own hands and go after Schwartz. I didn't want to lose you as well."

"You lied to me all these years!" Bryn shouted. "You told me Mum had died when her ship got smashed on the rocks in a storm. You told me!"

"And if I'd told you the truth would it have helped?" said Gawain, trying to hold back his anger. "It wouldn't have brought Marie back and I would have had to have told you and probably everyone else the truth about where I come from." He looked calmer. "But now these two girls – sorry, *ladies* – have, yet again, become involved in my life, so now would seem the right time for you to know everything and for me to put a stop to Schwartz once and for all.

"And revenge?" I offered hopefully.

"Of course!" said Gawain who laughed without humour. "Revenge for the death of my Marie and for ruining Bryn's life. But also revenge for the poor villagers and their families that Schwartz senselessly murdered in Camelot. They lost everything while he escaped to cause more trouble here."

"Are you really my father?" said Bryn. "I don't care about Schwartz and where he came from, but I do care that nothing I believed about you is the truth. You're a fraud and that's all you are!" Bryn turned, slammed the study door and ran out of the house with tears streaming down his face.

Gawain was about to follow, but Neets put an arm out to stop him.

"Leave him," she said gently. "He needs time to think and what he's just heard won't make that any easier. Leave him for half an hour and then I'll go to him. I think I know where he'll be."

I cast a sidelong glance at my cousin. Even I quite

fancied Bryn in a hunk sort of way, but it didn't take much to see Neets was smitten big time. All the telltale signs were there – stars in the eyes, quiver in the voice, volunteering for impossible missions, trying to impress the future father-in-law. Poor cow, I thought, I'll deal with her later. I turned my attention back to Gawain.

"So, how do you reckon to smash the Black Kni… sorry, Schwartz then?" I said it with what I believed to be overpowering tact and diplomacy. "Kick him where it hurts, take him back to be executed in Camelot, or just kill him?"

"I'm sorry?" With difficulty Gawain turned his attention away from the disappearing Bryn. "It's not as simple as that. If I did take him back to Camelot then I'd be changing history, and if I took him anywhere else it could leave an unexplainable Schwartz-shaped footprint. Besides, the Portals Merlin gave us are one-way only. They won't return us to Camelot. We can go anywhere else, but not Camelot."

"One of Neets's temporal anemones," I said. "So what are you going to do then?"

"Win, my young friend," said a grim Gawain as he unsheathed his sword. "I'm going to win and end this once and for all."

Neets followed Bryn at a discrete distance and unseen by both of them I brought up the rear. I quickened my pace and being younger and a lot more athletic I managed to get to the Salt House before either of them and crouched under a bush that gave no shelter from the rain, but at least hid me.

I watched Bryn as he slipped and staggered over the seaweed-covered rocks. Knowing the area like the back of his hand probably didn't help much in the dark, because like most people he could only describe the back of his hand as being pink, a bit hairy, and covered in veins. He reached the grassy slope that led to the bottom of the cliff and stood for a moment gulping in air, while behind him was the shape of the Salt House, though now there was no eerie light shining from inside. The look on his face told me the pain he felt at being lied to all these years by the only parent he knew and his stomach must have been churning. He looked very, very lonely as he sat on the soaking earth.

A muffled cough behind him was ignored along with so many other noises in the wind. Neets laid a hand on his shoulder and sat down beside him. For a couple of minutes she said nothing, presumably hoping that Bryn would break the silence, but he seemed too deeply absorbed in his thoughts and unless they were going to sit speechless until dawn it was going to be up to my cousin to make the first move.

"Your father loves you," she said eventually.

"I know," said Bryn.

"He must have wanted to tell you everything so

many times, but having lost his wife he wanted to keep you safe from any harm. He couldn't bear to lose you too."

"I know."

"But you're going to the Black Knight, to Schwartz, aren't you?" Unita sounded pretty certain, but it was still a question. "You're going to betray your own father." She spoke without emotion as though explaining a minor plot in a book.

Bryn looked devastated. "You think I could do that? You of all people." I waited for the next 'I...' bit, but he didn't say it.

"What are you going to do then?" Neets sounded confused and I have to admit so was I. "Whatever it is, I want to help, Bryn. I know what you must be going through." I waited for her to say the 'I...' words, but like Bryn she kept them locked away and shut up. The two unspoken sentences drifted away in the wind, but when a clap of thunder exploded directly overhead, Neets grabbed Bryn's hand and the young Welshman made no move to reclaim it. I felt the need for the non-existent sick bag yet again.

Seconds became minutes, but probably seemed to last the eternity of a moment for the two of them.

Bryn broke the magic of the silence. "Will you meet me here tomorrow night?"

"Why?" It seemed a silly question, but Neets was nearly a woman and probably wanted Bryn to tell her.

He hesitated. "Because I want you to." Then he

added, "I really would like you to, please. Besides, I'm going to Schwartz to try to get information for my father, not to betray him and if I can find out for sure where the wreckers are going to operate tomorrow night then my dad will be able to capture the lot. And ... and I like you."

Outwardly Neets smiled serenely. But I knew my cousin, and I could see that inwardly she leapt to her feet, gave a whoop of delight and reacted very much like Arthur had when he'd discovered Merlin was really a woman. "Very well, Bryn," she said calmly. "If that's what you'd like I'll be here at eight o'clock tomorrow night. Don't be late. Now go if you must."

Bryn stood up and helped Neets to her feet. He was still holding her hand and showed no sign of letting go. I wondered if this was going to be the right moment for their first kiss, or even for a quick peck on the cheek, but given the circumstances they formally shook hands. Then Neets nearly choked when I walked out from behind the bush.

"I don't know," I said shaking the surplus water out of my hair, "I leave you two alone for a few minutes and you go all romantic on me. Plus you make plans to deliver yourself on a plate to Schwartz. And you think it's all fine, Neets. Bryn, you're a fine pair. What makes you think Schwartz will believe you hate your dad all of a sudden and spill the beans, boy?" I reckoned that might shake him up a bit. "After seventeen years you're suddenly on his side? I don't

101

think so."

"And what do you propose instead ... girl?"

Was that the best he could do?

"*I'll* go to him." I carried on before they could come to their senses and realise what I'd just said. "I'll go because I can make him believe me. He was vain in Camelot and he'll be the same here. He won't understand why I should hate him even though he's already tried to kill me once here. He'll think that I really must want to join his gang of thugs, just for the adventure of it. It's a street credibility thing ... boy."

Bryn and Neets still stared with their mouths open but gave the slightest of nods.

"So I'll be going, but meet me here at eight tomorrow night, like Bryn said. Then I can tell you where the wreckers will be. On the other hand, if I'm not here, get Gawain to rescue me because I'll probably need it! With my luck I'll be chained to those rings in the Salt House!"

Before they could answer I turned and walked into the night up the muddy cliff path towards the wreckers' stronghold and an uncertain reception. I must have been mad!

I stopped near the cliff top and by the light of their storm lantern watched Neets and Bryn disappear into the darkness back to the manor house. I could have been mistaken but it looked to me as though Neets was floating on a cloud of happiness. Poor cow.

Chapter Seven

The Wrecker's Lair and Several Ways to Die

I struggled up the path to the top of the cliffs not daring to look back in case I chickened out and decided to follow the lovebirds back to Gawain's house.

The storm was less furious than before and the rain had slowed to a steady drizzle. The moon appeared as a dull glow through the clouds, but gave little light to see by, so I used instinct, plus old mumbled instructions from Bryn and the unreliable back of my hand, to avoid the gorse bushes and unseen rabbit holes.

I soon passed the beacon where earlier we'd met up with Gawain and walked on towards the villages of Mewslade and Rhossili. Schwartz's house – most would call it a fortress – was perched on a small rise set back from the headland and gave excellent advance warning of any unwelcome visitors. To Schwartz these would have been Revenue Men, Redcoats, Gawain and his men, or people he owed money to. Welcome visitors were probably very few and far between and included, well, they were probably very few. I approached Schwartz's house with a feeling of extreme nervousness and stopped several feet from the gateway, standing with my arms and legs spread wide apart to show I had no concealed weapons, though I was sure that whoever was watching me was armed to the teeth.

I heard a *click* as the hammer of a flintlock musket was pulled back and I could almost feel the owner taking careful aim. A second *click* meant he was ready to fire and I knew that Schwartz's men in Camelot had a habit of firing arrows first and not even bothering to ask questions afterwards, except of course *I wonder who he was?* Here was probably the same and I dodged to one side, held up both hands and shouted at the top of my voice.

"Don't shoot! It's me Tertia. I want to see Mr

Schwartz and I think he'll want to see me." I stood very still and hoped the fact that the musket hadn't been fired yet meant that the guard was considering whether to let me in. Of course it could also have meant that the gunpowder in the firing pan had got wet, in which case the guard was probably picking up a dry musket and would be shooting me any moment now. I screwed up my eyes and tried to make out any movement, but nothing stirred. I counted to ten then slowly moved into what little light there was in front of the gate keeping my arms outstretched so the guard would know I was no threat. There were still no shots.

"What do you want with Mr Schwartz? He don't like visitors." The unseen guard was probably running through a script and had no intention of deviating, which promised to make the conversation interesting as it progressed.

"First of all get me out of the rain and then I'll tell Mr Schwartz why I want to see him."

I'd completely thrown the guard. Not only had his target failed to answer the questions in the correct order, but I was now making demands. In desperation he shouted, "Open the gate!"

I started to walk forward and nearly died when a hand clamped on my shoulder and a voice whispered in my ear. "Careful, Tersh. Don't look too eager. I'm right behind you."

I nearly smacked her, but gave Neets a little hug instead. It seemed more ladylike. "What the heck are you doing here? You should be back home with Bryn and Gawain. Not risking both our lives."

"I told Bryn to go back home, make up with his dad and act his age. I also told him to leave the dangerous work to the professionals and that we'd see him tomorrow."

It sounded fair enough, except for the professionals bit and I wondered for a moment where my Inspector Smollett was, but only fleetingly. "I saw you walking back to the manor house. What possessed you to join me here?"

"Think about it. The Black Knight knew we did everything together in Camelot as Merl's Girls. Now he's Schwartz and knows we're both here so if only you turn up on his doorstep and say you think he's great and want to join him, he'll probably kill you. But if we *both* say we want to join him and have a good story to back it up then he may believe us."

"Ah! A credible story!" I spotted the flaw in Neets's plan. I watched nervously as the gates slowly opened. The guard was looking totally confused at our delay and was using one hand to pull the gate while trying to keep the pistol he held in his other hand levelled at our advancing figures. Beyond the entrance I could make out a large dimly lit courtyard and a group of men all of whom seemed to be heavily armed and staring in our direction. I licked my lips as we walked under the gate archway and into Schwartz's lair. It all seemed so simple, but then getting caught in the spider's web is always easy. Getting out is the problem.

I looked round the courtyard through the heavy drizzle, attempting for the moment to ignore Schwartz's men. Two oil lamps gave what little light there was, but I guessed that Schwartz would be keener to work in the dark rather than in broad daylight, or even any lamplight that might attract attention. Sweat poured off a line of horses in steaming clouds as they were led to their stables by a couple of men probably too old to go out wrecking anymore. Wooden barrels were stacked untidily as though having just arrived, while next to them was a pile of plunder that included bales of cotton and broken crates full of food ruined by sea water. It all pointed to recent activity and to my mind, severe mischief.

"Tertia and Unita. The two little tramps from Camelot." I hate being called little! "So in spite of my warnings you've come to see me." Schwartz stood in the entrance to his house looking as though he didn't have a care in the world. He leaned against the doorjamb and chewed a lamb bone as he studied us. "Why are you here? You and I have what you might call a history, both here and in Camelot." He laughed. "So I presume you're not here on a goodwill visit. Speak, or I should tell you that my men have some interesting ways of loosening tongues. They may even let you keep them in a jar afterwards."

I stared at Schwartz. This was the Black Knight who had tried to wreck Camelot, nearly killed my parents and laid waste to Neets's home. This was the man who for more than seventeen years had been terrorising the area around Port Eynon and wrecking any ship that strayed too close to the shore on a stormy night. We'd delivered ourselves like lambs to the slaughter and didn't even have a plausible story.

"I repeat, little girls," the man really knew how to hurt! "why are you here? Does the rest of your pathetic gang know you're here?" Schwartz was still smiling. "I rather think not, so it implies that either you and the rest have fallen out, or you're here to spy on me. Could it be you've at last discovered that the famous Sir Gawain is nothing but a vain, empty liar and been deceiving you all these years? Is that why you're here?"

God, he was clever. I'd never have thought all that out. I'd never noticed Schwartz's bald head in Camelot because he'd always worn a wig and now I was definitely facing the man who had tried to throw me from the church tower and who I'd seen riding away on his horse near Bryn's house. Somehow the lack of hair made the man look not only more villainous, but a lot less credible when he twisted the truth. I grinned up at the bald-headed gorilla, put my hands on my hips and tried to look brave.

"Yes, you're right." I almost shouted the words hoping that volume would make my anger seem more believable. Neets nodded. "Gawain blames you for everything that's gone wrong in his petty little life, including the death of his wife, which is crazy, because as everyone knows it was just a riding accident."

"Could have happened to anyone," said Neets. "He's definitely got it in for you."

"Ah yes. The beautiful Marie," Schwartz said with a theatrical sigh. "Such a tragedy. Her horse bolted in a storm not unlike tonight's and crashed over the cliffs into the sea ... or so I understand." He tossed the remains of the lamb bone into the courtyard for the dogs to fight over. "I would have thrown you from the church tower to stop you getting here, girl, so why would you still want to join me and why should I let you?"

He was asking bloody difficult questions and I decided that the only way to tackle the man was to avoid them and bluster. "Of course you would and I'd have done the same if I'd been you. I was an unknown quantity, so getting rid of me was the right choice. Good move, except I beat you. Remember? I let you get away too, because I didn't want you captured. I wanted you back here so I could join you. You're good at being bad and I ... I mean we ... can make you even more powerful."

Schwartz stared at us for what seemed an eternity and I had a feeling our lives hung by a thread – and not a very thick one at that. He pushed himself away from the doorpost and stood upright, towering above us in the shelter of the porch roof while we remained in the rain like drowned rats waiting for his decision. He grunted and nodded for us to follow him into the house.

The whole place had a medieval feel about it with no modern amenities. In the main hall a roaring log fire provided all the heat that was needed and light came mostly from bundles of rushes soaked in tar, which hung on the wall as lanterns. Much as we would have used back in Camelot. Time and technology seemed to have stopped for the Black Knight. The long tables were covered in scattered food of all kinds with jugs of ale for the thirsty.

"Sit down." Schwartz pointed to two wooden chairs near the fire, while he poured himself a glass of brandy and leaned against the mantelpiece. "I'll ask you again and this time, now that you've accepted my hospitality, I want a real answer." He put out a hand to silence me. "Personally I don't care what Gawain has, or hasn't done. I want to know why you're here. In other words what are you going to do for me?" The last words echoed round the room. Schwartz didn't seem to have shouted, but there was so much menace in the way he spoke.

"We came to help you," I said with a gulp.

"Help me?" Schwartz picked up an apple and bit deeply into the flesh. "What makes you think I need help from young pups like you?" He turned his head to one side and spat pips and pieces of core into the fire.

"We can let you know things," I almost squeaked in my nervousness, "like where Gawain is going to strike against you next."

"I already have informers in his household. What else?"

"Gawain's son Bryn is in love with me." I thought Neets was stretching things a bit there, "And he'll tell me anything I want to know about his father's plans."

"For instance we can let you know when the gentlemen smugglers are moving their goods," I added, appealing to both his vanity and his greed.

"Ah, now that may be of greater interest." Schwartz pushed himself upright and was paying more attention now he smelled easy pickings.

I knew there were two kinds of smuggler in the eighteenth century. The *gentlemen* only brought in those goods that were vastly over-taxed by the government and therefore priced beyond the reach of the average person. These items included brandy, tobacco, and strangely, tea. The gentleman smuggler was almost felt to be doing a community service and was held in high regard by everyone except, of course, the Revenue Men. The *devils* on the other hand concentrated on high-value items such as silks and occasionally slaves. Robbery, murder, and wrecking just made it easier. Schwartz was a devil.

He stretched out his hand. "In genteel circles we

111

would shake hands to settle our agreement. We'll do that, but I'll also warn you that if either of you makes any attempt to double cross me you will die." We stood up and shook hands, though after the casual way Schwartz had made his death threat my instinct was to run a mile.

"Tonight, you can sleep here in front of the fire with the dogs. Prove yourself to me and I'll reward you, just like I do the dogs." Schwartz threw the apple core into the fire and without a backward glance walked out of the hall into the courtyard.

We remained motionless for several minutes before I moved in front of the fire to dry off. I hate sleeping in wet clothes even when they're warm and reckoned I had a half an hour at least of steaming before I could curl up on my chair and close my eyes. Neets was bigger than me and would take longer to dry, though it has to be said she also started out being a lot wetter than me! In fact, my mind was racing and I ached in every muscle, so I knew that the chance of getting any sleep was less than a snowflake's chance in the fires of Hell. I smiled at Neets who was already curled up in her chair and snoring, then sank down on the floor in front of the hearth and slept soundly until dawn.

It wasn't so much the dog's tongue rasping on my cheek that woke me, it was more the boot prodding my stomach. The prods were becoming kicks as I groaned, eased myself into a sitting position and tried to avoid the early morning wake-up call. Neets was already rubbing her eyes and stretching the kinks out of her muscles. I stared at the bald-headed man looming over me and groaned again as Schwartz laughed.

"So, woken up at long last have you, girl?"

"My name's Tertia," I said sleepily and out of habit.

"Not yet it isn't. Until I say so, you're *girl*. Got it?"

I nodded. It was easier to nod than get another toe poke.

"Right, girl, follow me and bring your friend." Without another word Schwartz turned and walked out of the room. Neets and I followed him like obedient puppies. As we passed the tables I grabbed an apple and a cold pork chop, stuffing them in a pocket because by the look of it we'd already missed breakfast. Outside in the courtyard the barrels were still stacked in one corner, but most of the bales and plunder had disappeared. The wrecker and his men had obviously been busy during the night and the place looked swept.

Schwartz gave a humourless smile as he watched us taking in what we'd obviously been intended to see. Eventually he gave me a shove forward. "I haven't brought you here to look at what you saw last night. Today I'm going to show you other things and I may even show you how to fly." Schwartz threw his head back and laughed. Two of his men joined us as we walked out of the courtyard, across the headland and down a steep path overlooking the rocky bay far below. A morning mist and heavy dew made the stone track as slippery as a skating rink, though the view was certainly better. Schwartz stopped at the cliff edge.

"Look at that, wenches." *Girls* was far more preferable, but I didn't correct him. He pointed down at the sea far below. "Nice and calm, isn't it. Always is, after a storm like the one we had last night and there's hardly a ripple now." He picked up a stone and lobbed it, watching it arc into the sea. We heard the distant splash and saw the spreading ripples. "I call it the Leap of Faith and it's for those who cross me and therefore deserve to die. You two would have made a much bigger splash than that stone and if you double-cross me you still will. Believe it." I believed it and Neets gave a little squeak as our small procession made its way down the path. Personally I was highly relieved when the vertical drop became a gentle slope.

A few hundred yards ahead we came to a small bay that was a sheltered, sandy paradise now that it was low tide, but later would be hidden under several feet of churning water.

"Do you know what this is?" Schwartz said pointing at a large cave entrance that for some reason was almost completely bricked up. "This is Culver Hole, but nobody knows what it's for, or why it's all closed. Most think it's for pigeons."

For some reason we laughed and I remembered Reverend Lewis had mentioned Culver Hole as somewhere interesting.

"You hold onto that idea, girls, until I say different, but remember that whatever lies behind those bricks belongs to me, pigeons or not. Come with me, I have something else to show you."

In spite of his massive frame Schwartz leapt from rock to rock with the confidence of a mountain goat and it was as much as we could do to keep up with him let alone maintain our footing. The rocks at the base of Port Eynon Point were slippery from the storm the night before and the salt foam made it difficult to see what was rock and what was crevasse. Neets gave an involuntary cry as she lost her footing and slipped towards the broiling waters and jagged rocks far below. She desperately tried to grab an outcrop of rock, but missed it by inches.

"Not so fast, girl." Schwartz grabbed Neets's arm and hauled her back from the abyss. "I'll decide if and when you take the Leap of Faith. I'll not have you practicing." Before Neets could thank him Schwartz had turned and was striding round the point towards a distant building that we knew all too well.

When we reached the Salt House, Schwartz threw open the door and almost pushed us inside before locking it behind us with a very obvious click. The stillness and damp cold of the place was unnerving and the air was full of the tang of salt, though because the tide was at its lowest ebb the main salt puddling tank was empty (whatever puddling is). I knew we were in the puddling room, though, because there was a crudely painted sign with *Puddling Room* on it.

Schwartz led us down a mercifully small number of slippery stone steps until we stood on the even more slippery floor of the tank. I'd expected green slime and seaweed, but the smooth rocks gleamed in what little light there was and the salt crystals glistened in the gloom like tiny dull diamonds.

"Close your eyes," ordered Schwartz as he grabbed me by the arms. Neets meekly did as she was told. "I'm going to blindfold you both. I don't care how much you're fed up with Gawain, I still don't trust you. Stand still and stop struggling. I'm not going to hurt you, at least not yet." As he spoke Schwartz undid his neckerchief and tied it roughly around Neets's head, then spun her round, making sure she could see absolutely nothing and had no idea in what direction she couldn't see it. He turned to me and ripped the sleeve off my dress, which was better than the alternative of his old hanky.

We were pushed blindly along the tank floor, more concerned with not falling flat on our faces than with where he was taking us. I held my arms out in front of me as I shuffled along knowing a wall of some sort couldn't be more than a few feet away and I had no intention of getting a bloody nose. I heard a click and the sound of heavy movement.

"Duck down," Schwartz put a hand on each of our heads, "and keep those blindfolds over your eyes until

I say you can take them off." I wasn't going to argue and instinctively stooped as I was pushed forward no more than five or six feet. "You can stand up now, girl, and uncover your eyes. You too, Unita."

I looked around not knowing what I expected to see. Schwartz was holding an old oil lamp high above his head and pointing towards a short flight of steps carved into the rock at the end of what was presumably an old bricked-off sea cave. On the wall below the steps were two relatively new looking iron rings fastened to the rock at waist height. Schwartz smiled when he saw me looking at them. Neets was pointing excitedly at the rings because she'd seen them before.

"Unwanted pests get fastened to those two," he said, enjoying our reaction, "then at high tide when the sea comes pouring in and fills this cave the pests are no longer a nuisance. Some whimper and cry and some scream, but nobody can hear them. Most of the salt puddlers don't even know about this cave and the noise of the sea drowns out everything." He laughed at the look on Neets's face. "Are you a pest, Unita? Shall I leave you here until tomorrow, or keep the rings empty for other pests I might need to destroy?" He paused as though thinking through a complex problem. "Yes I believe that's what I'll do. It's your lucky day, girls. Follow me."

I glanced at the two rings and had a pretty good idea what the future held for us. Schwartz was already at the top of the steps making us hurry after him before the light from the lamp disappeared completely. After the last step, even I had to stoop to follow the giant Schwartz into a tunnel that looked anything but natural and as though it had been only recently carved out of the living rock. To my relief, rock soon gave way to earth and the ceiling gradually rose to head height until even Schwartz could walk upright without swearing every ten paces. That only left the cold, the damp, and the incredibly slippery earth to contend with. I couldn't help wondering why on earth Schwartz hadn't bothered to get his men to put down some nice dry sand if he was so all-powerful. But maybe he was also plain thick.

"We're nearly there," said Schwartz, breaking the silence. "Keep up and stop lagging behind, or I'll leave you both down here to consider your lack of a future."

We hurried forward, catching up with the wrecker just as he opened a massive wooden door and entered a large brick-lined room. My mouth dropped open as I stared at the vast treasure trove that filled every inch of the floor. Everything was piled up without any thought for what they were, or their value and I couldn't help thinking that whoever had done the storing had lost all interest a long time ago. One item attracted my attention more than any other, mostly because of the ultraviolet glow coming from its centre. Schwartz's portable Time Portal stood in a corner and was on standby.

"You've both seen one of these before," said Schwartz when he saw where I was looking. "Gawain has one in his cellar, as if you didn't know. Tertia, I saw you and his brat escaping through it when I got into their house to smash his Portal. That's when I realised you'd found me and I'd have to deal with you more permanently. But maybe you've both come to your senses and if you really want to join me I might let you live a little longer … but not too long," I heard him mutter the last words and shuddered.

We followed Schwartz into the cave the wrecker used as a treasure store and this time I took a closer look at our surroundings. The whole place was piled high with treasure the gang had looted in seventeen years of wrecking and smuggling. Bales of silk lay open and rotting, bags of gems and money lay scattered and ignored, bottles of exotic perfumes were opened and useless, and yet barrels of rum and brandy lay neatly stacked in a corner.

Schwartz glanced at me. "This is nothing," he said with a sneer. "These are the discarded toys my men bring back after a night's work. What do I need with this trash? It means nothing, except to give me power and impress my small army."

"But if you don't want anything here," I said, "why wreck the ships? Why kill the sailors?"

"I just told you, girl. An army, even a small one means power, but it's a power that needs to be fed and my men need to know I'm invincible. I lead them to riches and glory and they follow me blindly, although often I have to admit it's because of what's in those barrels." Schwartz laughed. "Come over here and I'll show you something special."

Schwartz walked over to a door that had one of the largest locks I've ever seen, pulled a massive key from his coat pocket, and opened the lock almost with what looked like reverence. The room beyond was clean, well lit, and contained the most stunning works of art in existence.

Oil and watercolour paintings from every century, past and future, lined the walls and statues in nearly every precious metal and type of stone stood on the floor, or were mounted on plinths. Treasures, rare to the point of being unique, were displayed in cabinets that themselves were works of art. The entire vast room was a connoisseur's paradise.

Schwartz held up his lamp so that we could see right into the farthest corner. "Impressed?" Pride bubbled in his voice. "This is just the first room. The other four are larger and hold my real treasures."

He walked over to the statue of a woman. She wasn't wearing much above her waist and for some reason had no arms, but there was something about her that made me stand staring with my mouth open.

"The real Venus de Milo," said Schwartz proudly. "The one in the Louvre is a copy. I stole the original years ago and rather than admit they'd lost it the

French authorities had another one made and put in its place. That's happened with quite a few of the treasures I've stolen, like that painting over there." A woman with a slight smile on her face looked at us from a small frame. "That also came from the Louvre and it's another favourite of mine even though it's only painted on a piece of wood. They find the originals, I take them and they replace them with copies." Schwartz gently touched the Mona Lisa painting with his fingertips then looked at us. "Merlin's portable Portal lets me bring anything I want here. The only drawback is that the Portal won't let me go back to Camelot. Merlin saw to that. It also means Gawain's stuck here of course, which is some consolation."

"Are you saying you suddenly love beautiful things?" I said with hardly a trace of sarcasm, because I remembered how the Black Knight dealt with sarcastic people.

"I always did, even in Camelot."

"Beautiful things like Guinevere?" I could see I'd hit a nerve and was tempted to duck, but Schwartz made no comment, turned and was about to leave the room. He stopped when he saw me walk up to a small display in the middle of the cave that had obviously been reserved for a special purpose. Its plinth was made of marble, the display table was polished mahogany covered with plush red velvet and topped by what looked like a crystal eggcup. I decided the eggcup was probably of little value, so there was more than likely something missing, because even the oil lamps gave maximum effect to something that wasn't there.

"Down to the damned Gawain, young Tertia." Schwartz used my name again, though I was quite happy with *girl* especially from Schwartz and his many other favourite expletives. "That was to have been the greatest prize in my collection before that bloody bastard involved himself. I'd planned its theft for years and he managed to stop me."

I couldn't help wondering what could have been Schwartz's intended treasure and yet been so small. "Back in Camelot, Gawain was always stopping us from what we wanted to do as well," I said. "That's why we're here instead of with him." It made me cringe, but the wrecker seemed satisfied as he guided us back into the trash room. "Do we go back down the tunnel, or through the Portal?"

"Neither." Schwartz smiled, though a grinning skull would have had more humour. He took hold of my arm and pointed to the other end of the cave. "We go through that door and then up the steps into my house. We're home, girls. Or maybe I'll call you Unita and Tertia."

"But if this was what you wanted to show us, why'd we go all that way over the cliffs and rocks to get here." I decided that a bit of indignation might go down well.

"I needed to test you," said Schwartz. "You think I'm going to trust so-called friends of my greatest enemy just because you show up at my gate? I wanted you to see where traitors end up for one thing. I don't get many traitors and I promise you that no one has betrayed me twice."

"But what about Culver Hole?" Neets said. "Why take us all along there?"

"That was me showing off," admitted the human side of Schwartz's otherwise inhumane nature. "There are things that go on in there you'll never see. Besides, we needed to go past it to get to the Salt House and into the tunnel that brought us here." Schwartz opened a door, strode up the steps and pulled a lever high above the top stair as a door swung open letting light flood in from the room beyond. We had no choice but to follow him and I looked past Schwartz at the dining hall we'd left an hour or so earlier.

"We're back in your house," Neets said as we walked through the door at the top of the stairs. "We were in your cellars all the time and now we're back up in your place. Does this mean you trust us, because if you still don't would we have come back here the long way?" She looked at Schwartz pointedly. "Or only half the way?"

"I don't trust anybody, girl," Schwartz said without the slightest expression in his voice. "Not a single person. There are some people I nearly trust and there are others who would do well to keep out of my way."

This time his smile did have as much humour as a skull, though not a very happy one. "Why should I trust you more than any of the men who've been with me for years? Of course I don't, but you may prove to be useful."

"And if we're not?" inquired Neets, because she had to ask.

"There's always the quick Leap of Faith from the cliff top into the sea, or the slow manacled tidal death in the Salt House. Take your pick."

"I think we may be useful."

"I thought you might." Schwartz walked over to a table and poured himself a mug of wine. He nodded to both of us, offering whatever we might want from the breakfast table although there was very little left especially in the way of food. I shook my head. The apple I'd eaten earlier would do until lunchtime and I still had the cold chop. Neets grabbed a bread roll and stuffed it in her mouth. "You've had a good night's sleep, food and drink, an invigorating walk and you've seen my treasures. Now it's payback time. Go to the stables and muck out the horses. Be quick, because we'll be busy tonight."

"Why?" I asked, my curiosity getting the better of my common sense. "What's going to happen?"

Schwartz perched on one of the tables, looked at me and scratched his chin. "A storm, that's what. Probably one of the biggest this year and the tide is at its highest. All that adds up to ships being wrecked and us getting rich."

"But they'll avoid this coast like the plague."

"Not if we put our beacons out in the right places. They'll be lining up to be smashed on the rocks." Schwartz laughed.

"Whereabouts are we putting the beacons? There can't be many places left you haven't used." I was pushing my luck, but if I didn't ask then we'd never be told.

Schwartz gave me a look that not only had suspicion, but a danger warning written all over it. "Very well," he said slowly as he pushed himself upright from the table. He put his mug down as though deep in thought. "It's to be the Crabart and if there are soldiers, or Revenue Men ready to meet us, I'll know where they got their information. Remember the Leap of Faith, young Tertia, especially if you want to become *old* Tertia."

Bryn had told us the Crabart was one of the most dangerous causeways on any coast, let alone in South Wales. It separated the mainland from the Worm's Head, three long, thin islands that stretched half a mile out to sea, and at low tide was a rocky seaweed-strewn pathway for the wary. At high water the tidal rip raced over the Crabart causeway destroying any ship looking for a shortcut and many had simply disappeared after being smashed to matchwood.

So it was to be the Crabart, and tonight.

"Now go and work and I don't want to see you

again until this evening."

We walked over to the stables and I smiled to myself. We had news that could destroy the man who had terrorised the coast and killed Bryn's mother. It was weird, but could Schwartz be so naive as to think we'd believed his version of Marie's death, or did the man really believe we disliked Gawain so much? It seemed so.

We mucked the stables for an hour, crept out of Schwartz's lair when no one was looking, and made a run for it.

Chapter Eight

Breakfast, Lunch and Gawain's story

We got back to Port Eynon at half past nine in the morning and I realised just how early the Black Knight had woken us with his kicks, though I have to admit I was beginning to think of him just as a nasty piece of work called Schwartz in spite of all he did to us and our families in Camelot.

I wanted to sort out a few things before we went back to Bryn's house and got bombarded with the inevitable loads of questions, but I also needed a long hot bath and a really big breakfast. Neets didn't argue even though I suspected she was itching to get back to her Bryn. Poor cow!

Port Eynon's inn can't have had much passing trade and welcomed us with open arms, especially when we mentioned we were staying with the Lewis family and the bill should go to them. An hour later we ordered two full English breakfasts, with everything, twice ... each, and got the Welsh version which had sausage, eggs, bacon, mushrooms, mussels, tomato and fried bread, and as a special treat a good helping of a local seaweed called lava bread. Close your eyes and hold your nose, I decided, then it probably won't taste too bad, especially as I was ravenously hungry and my last meal had been a vastly overpriced bread roll in the *Olé Grill* and a Schwartz apple. I had thirds and Neets had fourths.

When the plates were empty with probably no need to wash them we sat at a table in the bar and made notes on what we knew so far. This took up a whole page in one of Neets's detective notebooks. Most of this was our names, the case number, the date and where we were staying, plus details of the free breakfast in case we could claim it on our expenses. Then we made notes, which took up several pages of very small writing.

I paced up and down with my hands clasped behind my back doing an impression of Marlene doing an impression of Sherlock Holmes dictating to Dr Watson, while Neets pretended to be a detective and did a reasonable job.

"Right," I said starting my summary, "let's see what we've got. Both the Black Knight and Gawain are living here and are at each other's throats. They can't get back to Camelot with their Portals, but can travel elsewhere and transport objects. We can go back to Marlene with ours, but nowhere else. Lot of bloody use." I started ticking off on my fingers again. "Schwartz wanted to steal something small, but very valuable – query, a diamond – but Gawain stopped him. The wreckers are going to be on the Crabart tonight. Marie's two sisters are both working in Port Eynon and lots of people in this village seem to worship Gawain, or Lewis, as he's known here. Bryn's a hunk and you seem to be getting very friendly with him. Sorry, Neets." I couldn't help laughing at her blushes. "To cap it all, we still have a statue of Lord Nelson in Galahad's restaurant, and a young Welshman who seems to have been the focal point of everything and of course whose mum was killed sixteen years ago, but nobody's really sure how." I looked at Neets. "So how are we doing and what do we deduce from that lot then?"

Neets thumbed through her collection of notes, chewing on the end of her pencil. "Not much," she said at last. "Actually we probably know everything, but as to what it all means … I haven't got the foggiest, except that the villain is the bald-headed guy Schwartz, and the good guy is the famous and brave

Mr Lewis. Makes sense when you think about it because in my experience if there's no proof, the bald-headed guy always did it."

"Not bad," I said grudgingly. "Mind you, we also know Schwartz has a Time Portal in his cellar and that Gawain also has one that Bryn accidentally started, grabbing Nelson and me in the process."

"Don't forget he also managed to take Marble Arch and God knows where he's going to hide it in a place like this."

"Nelson's statue's a bit of a puzzle too," I said running my fingers through my hair. "The Portal must have been focused on it for some reason when Bryn flicked the switch." Back in Camelot, Marlene had developed PortalVision so she could see what was going on elsewhere in Time, although unfortunately it only worked from the main Portal in Merlin's cave. She'd even worked out a way of talking to Portal time travellers using a couple of old tin mugs as microphones and if Gawain could move statues, I wanted to know whether Marlene had taken out a patent on how to do it yet.

"Right," I said, "if we're all sorted, let's get up to the manor house and meet up with the good guys again."

"If I come with you," said a very familiar voice from behind me, "do you think Bryn's father will settle my hotel bill? They won't take my credit cards here."

I laughed and gave the shocked Inspector Smollett

a hug. "Hi, your Inspectorship. I wondered when you'd show your face. Don't worry, we'll fix it. We've got a sort of Bryn tab running." Before he could say anything else I led the way past the relieved tavern keeper and up to Gawain's manor house.

It seemed like only seconds after I banged on the door that it slowly opened as Mrs Jones, the housekeeper, peered out, then swung the door fully open with a shriek of delight.

"Thank the Lord you're safe, girls." She gathered Neets and me in her vast arms and could probably have swept up my inspector as well if she'd only seen him in time. "We were so worried about you when Bryn came back alone last night." She shooed us through the hallway and into the kitchens. "The master wanted to ride out and look for you, but Bryn persuaded him that you knew what you were doing. Did you, my dears?" She sat down in her large armchair and pointed at two smaller chairs for us. "And who's your very respectable-looking friend? I'm assuming you know him and he's not a vagrant wandered in for a cup of tea." Smollett stood fiddling with his hat in his hands, an uncomfortable grin on his face.

"This is Inspector Smollett, Mrs Jones," I said, standing up and bowing in his direction. "He saved me twice from a certain very high something when he had vertigo and he's been helping us as a professional copper." I paused. "Or at least he would have if he hadn't wandered off after we came to Port Eynon. Where *did* you vanish to, Mr Inspector?"

"Never mind," said Mrs Jones. "He's a friend of yours. That's all that matters. A lot has also happened at this end and you look as though you could do with a cup of Merl Grey tea, Mr Inspector." I reckoned Bryn hadn't been idle after all and must have passed on the recipe the previous night.

Smollett was about to say we'd just had breakfast, but I managed to stop him in time with a well-aimed kick on the shins. I hadn't had a decent cup of Merl Grey for centuries and if Mrs Jones had managed to brew one I was prepared to kill for a pot. As Neets and I sat down the kitchen became a hive of activity, mostly of teacups being raised and food being eaten.

Mrs Jones was taking it all in her stride as though time travellers dropped into her kitchen on a regular basis. Of course, Gawain already had and it was just a shame she hadn't known all about him from the outset, as it would have saved a lot of trouble.

"You're welcome in my kitchen, all three of you," the housekeeper said as she studied the inspector's face. He sat down and nursed the cup of Merl Grey tea Mrs Jones had poured for him. "You're welcome to share my fire and its warmth." Neets and I stood and bowed, recognising what Mrs Jones was saying was a centuries-old cook's welcome. "You're welcome to my food and the energy it'll give you." We bowed again. "And to the drink that'll slake your driest thirst." We bowed one last time. "But keep your thieving hands off my lunch. I'm a growing woman and need all the nourishment I can get!" The housekeeper laughed until her chins quivered and her stomach vibrated in protest. We joined in out of politeness before sitting down again.

Two cups of Merl Grey and a slice of toast later I remembered that Smollett still hadn't told us where he'd been, even though we'd paid his tavern bill. Well Bryn had, or rather would, when we told him.

"Your Inspectorship." I was determined he wasn't going to get away with keeping a secret. After all I couldn't, so why should he. "There's no need to be shy. We're all people of the world, except for Neets of course 'cos she thinks she's in love or something. What happened to you after we split up?"

"I was told not to tell you too much and preferably nothing."

"Who by?" I asked, suspecting I already knew the answer.

"Marlene."

"She came here after all and didn't even bother to see us?"

"No, she dragged me back to the future so I could brief her, but she also wanted to tell me a couple of things she said would prove useful here later."

"And?" inquired Neets impatiently. Being in love does that to you.

"She said I wasn't to tell you or it could all go

wrong. She refused to say what it meant but indicated we'd understand when we needed to. Then she sent me back here."

I looked at Neets and winked. "Blimey, Marlene is such a crafty witch!"

"You don't seem particularly worried." Neets passed me her cup to put in the washing bowl and it occurred to me she hadn't mentioned the wonderful Bryn for well over fifteen minutes now.

"I'm not," I replied. "Right now we've got more important things to do than play games with Marlene. I wondered why she let us come on our own and it turns out she's sorting out little games for us to play from the comfort of her own restaurant. Serve her right if Galahad puts his prices up!" I turned to my favourite copper. "So, Mr Inspector, looks like you'll have to keep your secret and I know how tough that's going to be. You'll just have to tell us when the time's right and none of us will be any the wiser except you."

"Where's Bryn?" Neets looked around as though he might be hiding. She may have lasted fifteen minutes, but I knew she'd never crack the twenty mark.

"He's out with the master." Mrs Jones was obviously beginning to sense it might be approaching lunchtime and was eyeing the assorted cold meats piled high on the large wooden table. "They should be back from their ride soon. Maybe we should have a quick lunch before they arrive?" She half rose from her seat when a distant door slammed shut and the voice of Gawain drifted down the corridor to the kitchen, followed by the man himself and his son. Neets's little face lit up like a wrecker's beacon as Bryn walked in. Poor cow, as I might have already said.

"You're back!" shouted Bryn, presumably in case we weren't aware of the fact, as he made a beeline for Neets. "My dad and I were really worried when you didn't come home last night. Well, my dad was mostly. I wasn't." Poor old Neets's face fell a mile and the beacon almost went out. "I knew you'd be braver and more resourceful than any of us and would easily outwit Schwartz." Neets nearly purred. "We've just been out looking for you both along the coast, but I told my dad you'd probably be back here by now, and so you are." Neets was nodding so enthusiastically I was ready to catch her head when it finally fell off. It was obvious too that Bryn and his father were friends again and that Bryn had come to terms with the fact his father was not a Port Eynon local, but a knight of Arthur's Round Table from a thousand years earlier.

Gawain picked up a chicken leg from the table, then stood in front of us with his back to the fire until his trousers started to gently steam from the morning showers. "What possessed the two of you to go to Schwartz? The man's a murdering thug and I wouldn't have been surprised if he'd killed you just because you came from Camelot. As the Black Knight, the man had no redeeming features and as Schwartz he can't even claim to be a knight."

Neets put up her hand hesitantly because you probably have to do that to prospective fathers-in-law. "He does collect nice things. He's got some lovely paintings and jewels and things stored in his cellars."

"Ah, yes," said Gawain, "his stolen hoard of art treasures, all hidden from the light of day where no one can see them, especially the real owners. I stopped him stealing the largest diamond in the world and he'll never forgive me for that."

"He sort of told us and we saw where he was going to display it on a special plinth."

"So, I accept the fact you went to his house and by some miracle managed to get back alive. Tell me what happened." He walked away from the fire and picked up another chicken leg. "But let's all eat while you do." Mrs Jones moved liked greased lightning and the rest of us followed in her wake.

While the others nibbled, munched, and swallowed, Neets and I described our reception at Schwartz's fortified house and what he'd shown us that morning. We tried to leave out nothing, though I didn't mention Neets's snoring to limit her blushes. Bryn was probably going to have to find that out for himself. When I mentioned the wreckers were going to the Crabart that night Gawain nearly dropped his goblet of wine.

"You're sure?" he said, putting a hand on my shoulder. "You're sure Schwartz said the Crabart? I have spies in his house and in all these years they've never managed to find out where he's going to be wrecking. If what you say is true then this could be my best chance of catching him red-handed."

"But what if he lied to us?" I said. "What if he told us it was the Crabart so we would tell you and he could go somewhere else knowing you wouldn't be there?"

"That's not Schwartz. He would either double-think you so you were meant to believe it wouldn't be the Crabart when in fact it is, or just as likely because of his arrogance he wouldn't believe that you could betray him. Either way I'm sure it'll be the Crabart. The man is trapped by his own twisted stupidity." Gawain looked animated. "I think I've got him." He realised he was still gripping my shoulder and released it with a triumphant smile. "Sorry."

"No problem." I did a little bit of massaging to get the blood flowing again. "So where do we go from here?"

"I don't know where we go," said Mrs Jones through a mouthful of bread and sliced beef, "and I'm still not even sure where you all come from." She munched thoughtfully. "On the other hand you're all lovely people, even you Mr Inspector Smollett, and I really don't care, just so long as we beat the man who killed my sister."

"Thank you, Mrs Jones." Gawain smiled. "We'll get him, but he'll answer for many more crimes than

Marie's death." He turned to me, nodded towards Neets and Bryn and gave a questioning shrug.

I gave an answering shrug back. "Neets has got herself a boyfriend," I said, combined with a look of *can you believe it* written all over my face. "She and Bryn are sort of like an item." Neets heard my last comment and I wondered how similar Neets's deepening blush was to Marlene's hair colour and why fancying someone was so funny and yet so embarrassing at the same time. A bit like someone's knickers falling down in the middle of a crowded room.

"Unita's a nice girl," said Gawain. "Bryn could do worse."

I agreed, then realised that Gawain was looking at me. Huh! I changed the subject. "Why haven't you mounted a full attack on Schwartz before now? You've had reason enough and you're the magistrate round here."

"All the more reason why I should abide by the law. I need proof or I'll be no better than him. I need to catch the man red-handed and what you've done last night and today may just give me the proof I need. By the way, Bryn tells me you arrived through the Portal in my cellars."

"Yes," I said, "but I'd suggest you get the thing bricked up when all this is over, or it'll only cause more trouble."

"I fully intend to. But right now I suggest we all

have a restful day, because tonight is going to be long and hard."

I was beginning to understand why so many people were prepared to follow Gawain wherever he led them. It wasn't blind faith and it certainly wasn't stupidity, it was because he had the knack of making them trust him completely.

"We'll help you in any way we can," I said at last, and added that the Temporal Detective Agency was at his disposal. After all, a bit of advertising never did anyone any harm. "And please don't worry about us. We can take care of ourselves, Sir Gawain Lewis. By the way, what *do* you want us to call you? To Neets and me you'll always be Gawain, but to everyone else here you're Mr Lewis."

Gawain looked at me and smiled. "I was Sir Gawain the White Knight for many happy years in Camelot and the experiences I had will always remain with me. However for the past eighteen years I've been Mr Lewis and most people here only know me as that. For the sake of my son, my friends in Port Eynon and because I intend remaining here for the rest of my life, I'll be Mr Lewis from now on."

Lunch didn't last very long. Mrs Jones saw to that.

Some cold meats between two slices of buttered bread and it was all gone in five minutes. It was the sort of meal that someone would invent one day and name after themselves, but somehow two rounds of Mrs Jones just didn't have the right ring about it, so the sandwich would have to wait another thirty odd years.

"Right, Mr Lewis," I said after all the plates had been neatly stacked. They could be washed later. "The statue. I want the truth from beginning to end. I've already worked out some of it for myself so I'll spot it if you lie, okay?"

"Very well." Lewis sat down in Mrs Jones's favourite chair, stretched his legs and put his hands behind his neck. "Where shall I start?"

"I told you where, at the beginning. Actually you can start by telling me where your Mrs Jones and my Inspector Smollett have gone." I looked around as though they might be hiding under the kitchen table like sniggering kids. "I didn't see them go."

"I've no idea," replied Lewis. "They probably went for a walk."

"Mrs Jones doesn't look like the rambling kind to me," I said as I sat down next to Lewis, "more the rolling kind. Never mind, please continue … from the beginning."

Lewis cleared his throat and for a brief time became Gawain again.

"When Schwartz arrived in Port Eynon he started a wrecking gang and used his Portal to steal treasures from wherever he chose. He went for anything that was incredibly rare, or totally unique, and one of my informants told me about the treasure hoard deep beneath Schwartz's house that only the wrecker himself is allowed to see. My informant, a personal friend, was thrown over what Schwartz calls his *Leap of Faith* and I never saw him again. One day another of my men discovered that Schwartz planned to steal the Koh-i-noor, one of the world's largest diamonds and certainly the most notorious, from the Crown Jewels collection in the Tower of London. You may not have heard of it because it wasn't given to Queen Victoria until the 1850s. It was totally unique in its size and brilliance, so of course Schwartz just had to have it."

Lewis sipped from a goblet of wine. "I had to stop him, because he couldn't be allowed to continue stripping the world of its treasures so I decided that if I couldn't put a halt to his wrecking, then I would certainly stop his thieving." He leaned forward. "I thought about it hard, Tertia, and the best way to stop a thief is to steal whatever he's after and put an exact copy in its place – a copy so good that he wouldn't be suspicious, at least not from a reasonable distance.

"Every evening for three months before I stole the diamond I travelled to the year 1867 and posed until dawn as a Beefeater guard at the Tower. Because I never did anything unusual everyone trusted me. I knew I had to steal the Koh-i-noor before the date Schwartz had fixed for his theft, so on one moonless night at three o'clock in the morning I left my post and replaced the diamond with an exact replica. That wasn't as easy as it sounds because the diamond was built into an ornate brooch, so I had to be very careful not to break the setting."

Lewis took another sip of wine and refilled our mugs.

"I have to admit the diamond was a thing of exquisite beauty," he continued, "and I was very tempted to keep it when the copy was in place, but that would have been inviting major problems if Schwartz ever found out what I'd done, not to mention the fact I suppose it would have been illegal. I knew I had to hide the original Koh-i-noor where Schwartz would never find it, and also make sure the replica was more carefully protected in the Tower of London. Let's face it, if I could steal it then Schwartz certainly could."

"Okay," I said, "so you stole the diamond, but I don't see what that's got to do with the statue, or me ending up on a pillar and getting wrapped up with Bryn." I paused then grinned mischievously. "Sorry, Neets. When I say *wrapped up with Bryn* I mean not so much wrapped, as involved with him. No not that either, because that's what you are in a … er, sort of way." The hole I was digging just got deeper.

Neets shot me an angry look. "Shut up, Tersh."

"I had to hide the diamond somewhere," Lewis continued, "and I'd already thought of the perfect place. I decided it had to be in the middle of London, totally inaccessible and where no one would ever think of looking for it."

142

"A statue on top of a hundred-and-fifty foot pillar," I said. "Very clever."

"I went forward in time a few years to when Admiral Lord Nelson's statue was being made by a Mr E H Baily and broke into his workshop. It was a matter of moments to gouge out one of the statue's eye sockets, put the Koh-i-noor in the hole and then cover it with a layer of paste. To be doubly sure, I put an eye patch over it soaked in wet cement and it looked as though it was part of the original statue unless you inspected it closely. I was certain Schwartz would never spot it from the ground and all I had to do was make sure that Mr E H Baily and his men were equally unobservant. When the statue was put on top of the column in Trafalgar Square, I knew that this time I'd beaten Schwartz."

"That's what I thought must have happened," I leaned forward, nodding.

"That's impossible. How could you have suspected the diamond was in Nelson's eye?" Lewis inquired suspiciously. "No one saw me put it in."

"Because if you know your history, Nelson never wore an eye-patch in his entire life, or so Marlene told me. So I always thought the fact his statue had one was very strange. But why didn't everything stop there?"

"Because I knew Schwartz wouldn't stop trying to steal the diamond," said Lewis. "Remember, I'd replaced the real diamond with the replica and as far as Schwartz was concerned it was still the original. I had to get the Tower of London authorities to move the Koh-i-noor to a safer place; somewhere that even Schwartz would give up and go home empty-handed. I couldn't just go up and tell people to put the jewels in much stronger cabinets, behind bars and in a better protected tower. Let's face it, they knew me as an ordinary Beefeater."

"So what did you do?" Unita asked Lewis as she looked at Bryn.

"I went back to the Tower disguised as an old woman and by stretching my arm between the bars protecting the diamond brooch, I nearly managed to get it out of the display before I was stopped. In those days the bars in front of the jewels were thick, but wide apart. They were a deterrent, but of little practical use."

"Weren't you arrested?"

"No. I was considered mad, given a strong cup of tea and sent packing with a warning. It taught them a lesson though and within a couple of days the whole collection was moved to another much more secure tower and placed behind bars so narrow even a child's hand couldn't get through. The Koh-i-noor diamond, or rather its replica, was safe and Schwartz finally gave up, though as you know he keeps a display cabinet free in his cellar to remind him of his one failure."

"Do you think he suspected you had something to do with the fact they moved the jewel collection?" I asked, already knowing the answer from Schwartz's own mouth.

"Almost certainly," said Lewis. "It would be too much of a coincidence and Schwartz doesn't believe in coincidences."

"Nor do we at the Agency," I said with feeling. "Which brings me to my next question, how did I get dragged into all this with Bryn? I reckon your son played around with the Time Portal in your cellar and the thing went haywire."

"Something like that," said Lewis. "I'd left the Portal controls focused on Nelson's Column so I could see that the statue was put into place by using the visual device and then check on it occasionally."

"That'll be Marlene's PortalVision," I said proudly.

"As far as I can tell, Bryn went into the Portal room against all my warnings and switched it on. Then like all inquisitive boys, he fiddled with the control knobs and probably put it onto full power just to see what would happen."

"Chaos," I said knowingly. "That's what happens when you get an idiot messing with things he doesn't understand." Neets was about to protest, then thought better of it. Bryn sat silent. "As a result we had Nelson's statue, Bryn, and me cluttering the Temporal Detective Agency office plus, had we known it, the Koh-i-noor diamond. As a bonus, of course, I also picked up my favourite copper Inspector Smollett." I stood up and slapped Lewis on the back.

"Come on, you're a man of action, or at least used to be. I've seen round your house as an undercover maid, admittedly only for a day, but I'd like to see it as it is now with furniture and people in it. Take me on a guided tour while Neets and Bryn do the washing up." My cousin gave a yelp of protest. "Remember, Neets, you're the maid and I'm the teacher. You can't expect a teacher to do the washing up!"

"You're absolutely right, Tertia," said Lewis as he walked out of the kitchen. "No tours and you can do the drying."

The dishes done, Neets and Bryn went for a stroll in the dunes, while Lewis and I stood on the Port Eynon cliff and looked at the calm waters gently slopping against the rocks far below. Oystercatchers skimmed over the waters and the seagulls wheeled high above, shrieking annoyance at their nests being disturbed by humans. It was an idyllic day and the sun shone high above as clouds gathered menacingly on the horizon.

"Lovely view," I said breaking the awkward silence. "If you shield your eyes you can see right over to Devon."

"You can at the moment," said Lewis, "but tonight will be a different matter. The low clouds will be as thick as fog and so inky black you won't see beyond your own nose. The wind will tear at your clothes and it'll feel as though the skin on your face is being peeled away layer by layer. The coming rain will make

146

it difficult to breathe and you'll think you're drowning." He paused and smiled. "Not a good night for walking the dogs."

"But a good night for wrecking ships?"

"One of the best," said Lewis. "One of the very best. Let's walk."

For the rest of the afternoon we made our way along the cliff path as the sun slowly moved towards the horizon. As we looked down into each bay, Lewis told me its history and whether Schwartz and his gang had ever used it as a wrecking point. Occasionally Lewis pointed out wooden spars, smashed planks of wood, and pieces of wreckage that may have been washed overboard from some distant ship, but were more likely to be the work of Schwartz. In one rocky bay I spotted the remains of a china doll. Its clothes were torn and one leg was missing, but I couldn't help wondering whether the owner had dropped it by accident or had become another victim of the wreckers. Weird thoughts for a fourteen-year-old, but over the past twenty-four hours I'd mentally aged rather a lot.

As the sun slid behind the cloud-filled horizon, turning the water into molten copper, Lewis stopped and stared out to sea as though searching for something. I put a hand on his and he turned, with a sad smile.

"I'm sorry," he said quietly, "every time I come here I look for my Marie. I have this feeling she's out there somewhere waiting for me to find her, but I don't know where to start looking." He sighed deeply. "Come on, let's get back home. It'll be dark in a couple of hours and we've a busy night ahead of us."

As Lewis started to walk towards Port Eynon, I didn't make any move to go with him and suspected from the look on his face he knew the reason. "There's something I have to do, or tonight will be a disaster," I said. "Schwartz needs to see me at his place sometime today, working or doing whatever, otherwise he'll know we've double-crossed him and change his wrecking plans. He has to think Neets and I have joined him for keeps, or at least that I have."

"What about Unita? Won't he think it strange she's not with you?"

I'd rather hoped for him to say something like: *"You brave girl. So young and yet the bravest person I know."* Nope. Straight onto Neets instead. Still, I thought, that's a future father-in-law for you! Unfazed, I continued. "Not really. In fact it might even look better if I tell him Neets ran back to you and Bryn, but I was true to my promise and stayed with him." I gave him a quick wave and started to trot towards Schwartz's lair.

"You brave girl. So young and yet the bravest person I know." Lewis shouted the words so they echoed round the cliffs and I knew I'd definitely arrived as a detective. I also knew in my heart that by morning the Temporal Detective Agency would have

148

solved everything to do with appearing statues, disappearing diamonds, and thieves living in the wrong century. I felt good.

Of course, if it all went wrong I'd be dead.

Chapter Nine

*Recruits, the Crabart and
Mrs Jones's Trap*

"Where've you been, girl?" I noticed that Schwartz wasn't using my name any more, though I suspected the wrecker never trusted anyone for more than an hour or two, including himself. "I know where you've been, so don't lie to me."

I paled and thought of the Leap of Faith. When I walked into the courtyard Schwartz had been standing outside the entrance to his house watching the distant storm intensify as it threatened to sweep in from the sea. I knew he was also keeping track of who walked in and out of the courtyard gate and why. I bunched my fists and got ready to fight as best I could or if necessary run like crazy.

"You've been moping around," Schwartz said before I could answer, "because your little friend turned chicken and ran. She did, didn't she?" I nodded, a bit annoyed that my well-crafted story was reduced to a single nod. "I thought so. Well don't!" The man's voice rose to a growl. "Remember that I use you and not the other way round."

For one awful moment I thought Schwartz must have had me followed.

"Sorry, sir," I said looking downcast, "I was looking forward to tonight so after I took Neets, I mean Unita, part of the way back to Port Eynon I finished in the stables then sneaked out and walked to Rhossili to look at the Crabart."

"And what did you see, girl?"

"Dead calm it was. The sea was right out and like a millpond. All the rocks on the causeway looked shiny with their seaweed and not a bit dangerous."

Schwartz nodded as he scanned the heavy storm clouds building up. "That's how I like people to think of my little bit of coastline, then they get careless. But tonight, now the storm's rising, there'll be murder, mayhem, and profit for us all." Schwartz could be very persuasive. "You'll be part of it, girl, and you'll play your part well, or you'll take the Leap."

"Yes, sir." I decided I'd said enough and shut up.

"Come inside, Tertia." Schwartz was becoming friendly again, at least for him, and my heart sank, because I liked him more as a villainous thug. I followed him into what would normally have been the sitting room, except it had no chairs and was full of miscellaneous plunder. Schwartz rubbed the glass of the main window and looked out. The storm clouds were racing in from the sea and within the hour would bring lashing, stinging rain in the howling wind. "Look out there, Tertia. The waves will be viciously unforgiving when they crash onto the coastline and in a couple of hours the Crabart causeway will be ready to smash any ship I entice there." The smile on his face at the destruction he was going to cause was sickening. Then his face clouded and seething anger replaced the smile. "Tonight will make up for all the trouble caused by Gawain both in Camelot and since I arrived in Port Eynon. Bryn's mother scorned me to marry him and the man has ruined too many of my profitable ventures. Now he'll pay." He turned from the window and stared at me. "Now to cap it all you and that other interfering brat have turned up again from Camelot. Tonight I'll eliminate Gawain at long last and show his boy Bryn the Leap of Faith from the top down to the very watery bottom. And if you and Unita have betrayed me you'll leap with him. This is going to be a very good night."

"You can trust me, sir." I was so good I almost believed it myself.

"Then get ready and meet me at the stables. We ride in one hour."

I walked off and tried to imagine what was going on in Schwartz's mind. I reckoned he'd be half inclined to change the wrecking site for tonight, just in case I spread the word, or if Neets was doing it right now. But then he would also reason that if I'd double-crossed him, Gawain would be too intelligent to fall for being misled about the Crabart and would think it had to be the next bay, which was Mewslade. In which case the obvious thing to do was to set up his wrecking operation on the Crabart, safe in the knowledge that his old enemy would be elsewhere.

The old double-think.

I walked through the courtyard archway and no one paid me any attention as I started to run towards Port Eynon. I'd done what I'd intended and Schwartz seemed satisfied that I was on his side and would join his plan of wrecking at the Crabart. Now it was up to Gawain and his people to finish the job.

As I made my way back through the village to Bryn's house, I turned off down a muddy side street just after the tavern and opened the large wooden door to the school. I looked into my class and was told they were writing an essay on where they would like to go if there was such a thing as time travel.

Amazingly they were doing it quietly and unsupervised. The Tertia effect! Miss Jones was in the other room doing a maths lesson and after a whispered conversation with me and a lot of nodding by her, she clapped her hands for attention while I went back into my classroom and told the kids to quickly join the others next door.

Miss Jones looked at the packed classroom with obvious pride and smiled at the eager faces arranged before her. Those children who didn't have seats were perched on desks and those who did sat on chairs craning round to see what was going on. We wanted to talk to them all without repeating ourselves, and saying things twice is something all teachers hate doing. Besides, we wanted a unanimous vote at the end of what was going to be a short speech. Miss Jones coughed for silence.

"Children, this week a new teacher started with us and I believe she has proved fairly popular. Am I right?" Nobody wanted to be the first to respond, but slowly there was a rising murmur of agreement. "Good. I know that Miss Tertia has told you some wonderful stories in her history and geography lessons, but I suspect you're too grown up to believe everything she said." Another slow murmur of agreement. "However, I have reason to believe there's more to our new teacher than meets the eye. For a start it would seem she's a detective." Another murmur this time of surprise went round the room and there was also the odd *What's a 'tectif?* "What's more she's on a case right now and if I'm not mistaken, and I very rarely am, she's encountering problems and needs help. My question to all of you is … do we help Miss Tertia? Yes, or no? Hands up."

It took less than two seconds for every hand to be raised.

"It may be dangerous and it'll be very dark."

All hands shot up again.

"And it'll be tonight."

It looked to me as though most kids had two hands raised this time. "That's my school," Miss Jones said to me proudly and as I left she started to outline to the children what they were going to do.

Back at the Lewis mansion I talked at length to Mrs Jones. "The master and his men are just getting ready to go, my dear," she said from her armchair by the fire. "Do you want to go with them?"

I told her what I intended to do and about my recent visit to her sister at the school. For a rather large person Mrs Jones could move quickly, but I was even faster as I grabbed the last sandwich left over from lunch.

"Do you think they're in real danger and will they need our help do you think?" I looked thoughtful and nodded through a mouthful of beef and mustard. "I thought so."

Blodwyn Jones put two fingers in her mouth, gave the most penetrating whistle I'd ever heard and within a minute the kitchen was full of older people. The only person missing was David, but then someone was going to have to look after the house. She stood in the middle of the floor with her arms folded, looking like a vast lighthouse, and stared at her scullery maids, parlour maids, kitchen wenches, and general servants with a smile. She was onto a winner.

"Boys and girls," she used the term loosely, "the master needs our help and I for one am not about to refuse him. Show me your weapons."

A variety of lethally-edged ladles, sharpened mops, spiked dusters, and wickedly tipped brushes were waved, or in some cases raised with difficulty. Blodwyn Jones laughed as she so often did. "Excellent. Then get the horse and cart hitched up because tonight we go to fight for the Lewis family."

Lewis had chosen horses for all of us. Bryn had the same chestnut mare that nuzzled against his cheek when he whispered in its ear and they looked as though they understood each other perfectly. Neets had been given a piebald pony that trotted up to her like an old friend.

"Used to be Bryn's," explained Lewis, "before he got too big for her. Now she'll only let someone Bryn trusts ride her. It seems he trusts you, Unita." He smiled that charismatic smile of his and Neets blushed in reply. Poor cow.

I looked at my donkey again and was about to protest when Lewis put a hand on my shoulder.

"Pedro isn't just a donkey, Tertia," he said gently. "He's the most surefooted animal on the entire Gower coast. He knows every inch of the headland and will look after you with more care than any boyfriend. He may be a donkey, but he saved my life many times. Tonight he belongs to you and I will ride another mount."

"He's yours?" I said in surprise. "You normally ride a donkey?"

"Certainly at night I do. During the day, of course, people expect me to ride on a large white stallion. That's him over there." He pointed towards a tall, proud horse that knew he was king of the stable. "But at night, I always trust myself to Pedro." He tickled the donkey behind its ears making it bray happily.

"In which case I thank you for your thoughtfulness." I bowed formally as befitted an apprentice wizard and detective who was addressing an ex-Knight of the Round Table.

"Then let's get mounted and go to meet our destinies."

From anyone else it would have got a chorus of groans, but from Lewis the words seemed exactly right. Outside the stables, Lewis's men were already on horseback, ready to follow their leader and I was amazed to see that one of them was an army Redcoat captain. I shot a questioning glance at Lewis because Redcoats were, after all, the enemy of smugglers and Lewis was reputedly one of the best.

"He's a good friend of mine," he explained. "In fact he was Marie's brother and is therefore Bryn's uncle, but that won't stop him arresting me if he thinks he should and I respect him for that. However, his hatred for Schwartz is as strong as mine, which means that tonight we're on the same side." The Redcoat gave me a salute, which I returned with a brief wave.

Lewis stood up in his stirrups and looked at the small mounted army that surrounded him. The cold rain was pouring down and the wind tore at our clothes, but there was no doubt all of us would follow him wherever he chose to lead.

"After tonight," he shouted above the noise of the storm, "there will be no more unnecessary deaths … after tonight." The last words were said with menace and after a pause he added, "Remember, Schwartz is mine."

As we rode through the village, curtains twitched aside and most householders gave a wave and some blew kisses. After all, it was their men who were riding out. Near the shore we turned to the right and headed up the rough track leading to the headland. The rain made everything slippery and in the dark it would have been easy to have taken the wrong turn and end up on the deadly rocks far below. Pedro was in the lead and the other mounts followed without hesitation.

At the end of the path the cliff top flattened out, though because we didn't dare use our lanterns we could see no more than a few feet in any direction. We heard the surf crashing on the rocks far below and in my imagination were the cries of sailors lost in the wind and desperate to avoid the splintering fate that awaited them. The Crabart was still some miles away and if we were to stop Schwartz we needed to hurry because the tide was coming in fast. I spurred Pedro into a trot and he responded with a slow canter while the horses kept up with us at a steady walk.

When we reached the toppled beacon where we'd first met our old friend from Camelot, Lewis called out a series of orders and four of his men dismounted. They put the beacon upright, filled it with dry wood and coals from their saddle bags before carefully lighting it using their flintlock pistols and tinder. Soon the beacon was a roaring fire in spite of the storm and the men remounted their horses.

"You're going to tell me why we've done that, aren't you?" I shouted.

"It's a decoy and a saviour," said Lewis, telling two of his men to remain with the beacon and make sure it stayed alight. "Schwartz will see it and think he's safe because we're waiting for him in the wrong place, but it'll confuse his men because they won't expect another beacon so near their own. Sailors will see it and stay away from shore because one beacon means safety, but two spells trouble."

"I knew there had to be a reason." I clicked my tongue and Pedro obediently moved towards Neets's piebald pony. "You be careful, my girl," I shouted into her ear. "Things are looking dangerous so make sure you watch where you're going and don't make an ass of yourself. Sorry, Pedro, no offence intended!" I turned and dropped back to the following horses.

We kept to the coastline until we passed the towering cliffs above Mewslade bay, picking our way slowly between the gorse bushes and the sudden outcrops of rock that loomed like giants through the rain. Surefooted Pedro led us down inclines so steep that I screwed my eyes tight shut, which was pretty pointless as I couldn't see more than a few feet anyway, and just to be sure I flung my arms round Pedro's neck and held on as though my life depended on it, which was indeed the case. After all, I'd stood on top of Nelson's column chatting to the pigeons, so I knew how to respect heights.

We reached the lower stretches of Butterslade without mishap and regrouped. Now that we were getting nearer to the Worm's Head, Lewis took the lead on his white stallion while Neets, Bryn, and I followed immediately behind. Lewis's most trusted lieutenants brought up the rear, because any ambush from the wreckers would take place from behind rather than at the front. I was quite happy to be surrounded by so many capable men and was whistling a tune that nobody could hear above the wind and wouldn't have recognised if they could.

At the westernmost corner of the Gower Peninsular

the high path stretched round the headland towards the Crabart and Schwartz's wreckers. The route was dark, steep, treacherous and seemed on occasions to double back on itself. Lewis shouted for absolute silence in case the wreckers had lookouts posted, but he needn't have worried, the roaring wind was so violent that none of his men heard him anyway. He held up his arm for attention and pointed forwards. His men followed in single file as he led us to the highest point of the cliffs overlooking Worm's Head – or at least where we knew the Head would be if only we could see it.

The rain had eased off to a driving drizzle, which at least meant visibility was better than zero and that as we dismounted Neets and I could see other people's noses and not just our own. We inched forward on our stomachs until we reached the brow of the cliff top and could make out the blurred action going on below. An older stomach crawled up beside us and a voice spoke just loud enough to be heard above the wind.

"So you were right," whispered Lewis, "Schwartz is here and it looks to me as though he's brought most of his men with him."

"Is that good?" said Neets, assuming it wasn't.

"It's good in that we can get all his gang in one go," Lewis said with a cynical laugh, "but it's bad in that there are rather a lot of the bastards, which might cause us a bit of a problem." We'd never heard

Gawain swear, even in Camelot, and I was quite shocked.

"So, what's the game plan, Gawain?" asked Neets, "Sorry, I mean Mr Lewis."

"You mean *Dad*," I muttered, very, very quietly.

Lewis looked at Neets. "I want the two of you to stay here and keep watch," he said at last. "Schwartz is no fool and he'll be half expecting us now that he knows Tertia may have betrayed him, purely by her absence. He'll try to attack us from the side, or maybe even the rear and I need some sharp eyes to watch out for him. The moment you see anything let me know. I'll leave one of my men to act as your messenger just in case."

Before either of us could protest, Lewis shuffled backwards on his stomach until he was sure he was over the brow of the hill and no longer visible to Schwartz's men. Brushing the dirt off his clothes he got up and walked back to organise the main attack.

Neets watched him open-mouthed, presumably because future dads shouldn't behave like that. "And after everything we've done for him and all we've been through! If he thinks I'm here just to be a darned lookout, he's got another think coming."

"Darn right. We didn't travel back in time to be a couple of spectators. After all the things we've been through a few pathetic wreckers shouldn't be too much of a problem for Merl's Girls."

We watched as Lewis and his men walked their

162

horses over the rise, covering their mounts' noses with their hands to stop them from making any noise.

"He wouldn't let me go either." Neets and I spun round and stared in bewilderment as Marlene walked over from what looked like a fading ultraviolet archway. She tucked a small remote control in her pocket. "He said it was going to be no place for a woman and especially for a dainty little thing like me." She put on a sour lemon face. "But I think he may have been joking there. He's a typical man, wrapped up in his own superiority complex, and totally blind as to how I could help him. I explained who I was and he even remembered me from my Camelot days, but it still cut no ice. He left me with this man for company and I presume he's also your so-called messenger." A grim looking man standing next to her nodded at us. "Personally I'm going to try a little bit of weather magic and see if I can't get the moon to shed some light on things. Care to give me a hand?"

"What on earth are you doing here?" Neets was the first to close her mouth and then open it again.

"What the bloody hell possessed you to come here?" I was the more blunt of the two of us. "We had a feeling you were poking round somewhere, especially after you grabbed my inspector, but you might have warned us."

"Oh, it's all right, dear. I'm only here for a quick visit. I was watching things through the PortalVision and I thought you could all do with a bit of moonlight, which is something our old friend the Black Knight would definitely not like. So I came to conjure some."

"But you said never to use magic when travelling in Time," said Neets.

"Oh, I know, dear, but I'm not actually travelling at the moment, I'm sort of stationary. Besides, you've got to keep your hand in and I rather think a little moonlight might hinder Schwartz, I believe that's his name here, and help our side. They'll think it's just a coincidence, because no one believes in magic anymore and wizards and witches only appear in stories to scare children."

"Speak for yourself," I said with feeling. "I'm real, I'm a wizard and I don't scare kids!"

"Yeah, just like half the children in your school class," said Neets. "Call yourself a *bona fide* teacher, Tersh!" Just for a change she was on the receiving end of the shin kicking.

"Ahem, when you've finished, girls," Marlene said haughtily. We all stood up, because if Lewis and his men were already way ahead of us and on their way to attack Schwartz there was little point in hugging the ground. "Anyway, I fancied some fresh air and Galahad's *Olé Grill* restaurant can get a bit huffy at times. Besides, he's started behaving strangely. I saw him examining that statue and fingering the eye patch. He was giggling in a most unknightly way too, so if you don't mind I'll get cracking with the grownup magic and you can go and amuse yourselves playing in the gorse bushes. I'll be gone in a few minutes." She turned away, raised her arms to the heavens with a look of intense concentration apparently trying to remember how the spell started.

I tried to think of a clever reply but ended up mumbling something incoherent that got lost in the wind. Neets was more for action than witty repartee.

"Tersh, this is how I see it. If Lewis and Schwartz are at each other's throats down there and Marlene's sorting out the weather up here, then there're two places that'll be empty. Lewis's house will be deserted except for Mrs Jones and her people." I quickly explained to Neets why they wouldn't be there either. "The other place is Schwartz's manor house. Nobody's been there except us because he keeps it too well guarded and he kept us well in sight, but I bet he'll have taken most of his men to the Crabart tonight."

I punched my cousin playfully on the arm. "And I know just the man to tell us the way. I've only been there from Port Eynon or by underground passage." I tilted my head towards the silent messenger.

"Mister," I said sweetly in my best *little girl asking for grown-up help* voice. "We've heard so much about that terrible Schwartz man, but it can't all be true. I've even heard that he's really a troll and lives in a cave and my friend here – gullible person that she is *(shin kick)* "Ow!" – was told that he's an evil sea demon and lives in the deep waters at the end of the Worm's Head. Is that right?"

The messenger didn't appear to be any less glum as he looked at the two of us to see who was the more stupid. He raised a hand and pointed inland towards where the hill of Cefyn Bryn separated the north from the south shores of the Gower peninsula. "Schwartz is no devil. He's a man like anyone else, but he is evil. He lives at the foot of that hill in a stone manor house with a wall right round it." He pointed into the gloom. "It's a big monstrosity of a place, guarded night and day and woe betide anyone who tries to get in without an invitation." He turned back to watch Marlene who was in full magical flow. She was much more fun.

Neets took the initiative. "He couldn't care about us, Tersh, and Marlene's wrapped up in the weather forecast. Let's get going."

"I heard that! You're old enough to look after yourselves now," hissed the wizard just loud enough for us to hear. "Go and do what you have to do, but be careful." She sang the last words without breaking her chant by even one note. "I'm off home in a minute."

We didn't hesitate. I stared into the night and could just make out the dark smudgy line of Cefyn Bryn against the inland horizon. Below it, about a half a mile away, would be Schwartz's lair, though right now it was still invisible. We broke into a stumbling trot dodging rocky outcrops and gorse bushes in the dark and trying not to slip on the muddy headland paths. The first two hundred yards were the trickiest, but once we climbed over the dry stone wall that edged the cliffs only the sheep got in the way.

Behind us I could hear occasional musket fire as Lewis launched his attack against the wreckers, though some of the shots must have come from Schwartz and his thugs. Men would be wounded and some would die on both sides and somehow, having brought them all together, I felt partly to blame. Then I heard voices in front of us and a few feet to our left. We crept over to the stone wall edging our field, pulled ourselves up level with the top, and quickly dove down again where we saw a number of men hurrying along a path leading to Rhossili village. Their swearing was terrible, but I was sure Neets wouldn't understand most of the words, unlike me and the Reverend Lewis who were far more worldly than the young lovebird. It was obvious the men were some of Schwartz's thugs making themselves scarce now that Lewis and his men were attacking and probably winning. Cowards aren't always thugs, but thugs will nearly always turn and run if they are losing, in my limited experience anyway.

"We can't let them get away with it that easily, Tersh." Neets was growing very bold all of a sudden.

"Dead right. Let's follow them. At least we can find out where they live, maybe even get their names and report them to Lewis." I climbed the wall, dropped down on the other side onto a stone path and couldn't help wondering why we'd been wading through a muddy field, only feet away from this nice dry trail. Some guide Lewis's messenger had been! Without thinking, I helped Neets down and we followed the voices and distant shadows as we got near to the village. I was pretty sure I knew what was going to happen when the men arrived, and wanted to be there to see it, having organised some of the plans.

We didn't have to wait long. I counted twenty shadows ahead which meant that a fairly large group of wreckers must have decided to leave Schwartz to his fate and merge back into the community, whether the community wanted them or not. They probably hadn't anticipated any trouble from the locals until they came up against Mrs Jones standing in the middle of the track with her arms crossed looking solid as a rock. She raised one hand.

"Don't think you're passing through here, boys, because you aren't. You'll either go back the way you came or surrender." She sounded so calm that she might have been offering a dinner choice of lamb or beef instead of an option of what was in effect life or death.

The wreckers looked at her in astonishment and those at the front burst out laughing encouraging their followers to do the same, but Mrs Jones remained steadfast, slowly lowering her hand.

"You going to stop us, old woman?" called out their leader, suddenly looking very brave. "You and whose army?"

"My army." Mr Lewis's servants walked out of the shadows and positioned themselves across the road beside Mrs Jones. They weren't all that menacing and most of them were on the wrong side of sixty, but they looked as though they meant business and were prepared to show why a cheese grater in the right hands could be a deadly weapon.

Even outnumbered the wreckers must have felt the odds were in their favour as they slowly moved forward holding their knives and cudgels in front of them. Most were grinning until several clicks on both sides of the road made them stop in their tracks. The sound was unmistakably muskets being cocked.

"Gentlemen, if you would be so kind as to drop your weapons and put your hands above your heads where I can see them." The Redcoat captain stood behind the wreckers, while his men surrounded them with their muskets loaded, aimed, and ready to fire. The clatter of weaponry falling to the ground was instantaneous and the fight was over before it had begun. Blodwyn Jones looked at me and sighed, and I knew what she meant, because some of the wreckers looked stupid enough to have mistaken age for an inability to crack a head with a rolling pin.

"Well done, everyone," she said beaming, "and to you and your men, brother, my special thanks." The

Redcoat captain bowed. "What will you do with this sorry lot?"

"They will answer for their crimes, sister, probably with their lives."

Mrs Jones nodded. "I admit some deserve their fate, but there are others who are no worse than average folk and given a chance may well mend their ways and contribute to our community. Heavens, it isn't as though we've got a surplus of men round here that we can afford to lose so many in one go."

The Redcoat captain didn't try to argue with his sister. "Very well, I'll leave enough of my men to keep a guard while I take the rest down to the Crabart to help wrap up things there. When I return I'll want to know who will go to Swansea prison with me and who will have a second chance."

Mrs Jones watched the soldiers march into the night then turned her attention to the wreckers who had lost their bullying courage. "Right, boys, I know which of you are the ringleaders so don't try to fool an old woman. Now the rest of you, who wants to live?"

A forest of hands shot up.

"It's amazing how most of you are basically really nice people deep down and we never knew it," she said with a laugh.

Chapter Ten

The Leap of Faith and Miss Jones to the Rescue

Neets and I followed the Redcoats back down the path for a couple of minutes, intending to cut across the field to Schwartz's house. I'd noticed a five-bar gate close to where we'd climbed the wall and saw no reason why I should scrape my shins yet again. I undid the latch and was about to swing the gate open when a dark figure loomed ahead of us barring our way.

171

"Marlene?" I said, hoping the figure wouldn't prove to be bald, male, and huge.

"Bryn?" said Neets, hoping for a hunk, and got her wish.

"Thank heavens you're safe, Unita." I'm sure Bryn meant to include me as well, but I'm not certain I really cared. "My dad and I were dead worried when we couldn't find you and especially when that Marlene woman disappeared through her Portal thing. Where are you going now?"

"To Schwartz's house," Neets said before I could stop her. This was Temporal Detective Agency business and Bryn was already getting too involved for my liking. "We want to look round his place while there's no one there. Do you want to join us?" Stupid question. Is Arthur king of Camelot? Or rather was he before he took up with the lovely Merl? Bryn grabbed the opportunity with both hands and then did the same to Neets as he helped her through the gate into the field. Typical man, I thought, as I followed them, closing the gate behind me.

"Wait a minute." I stopped. "You two go on and I'll catch up later. I've already had a personal tour of his house from the owner and besides, I want to see what's happening at the Crabart and make sure Schwartz is finished." I walked off towards the coastal cliffs before the other two could protest, but the way they floated across the field hand in hand made me realise they probably wouldn't notice if I was with them or not anyway. Not that I cared ... honest.

The sound of distant musket fire and the odd scream told me the fight was at its peak and probably nearing its end one way or the other. I could see the odd stab of flame from the guns as they fired, and I used them to tell me which way to go, though as they all looked alike I just hoped I'd chosen the right side's guns.

I watched as Lewis and his men dropped back allowing Schwartz's thugs to follow them screaming up the hill ready for the kill, but what the wreckers hadn't seen was the trap being sprung as more of Lewis's men emerged from the sides and surrounded them. Lewis called for a cease fire, offering mercy to those who put down their weapons and certain death to those who wanted to fight on. Most of the thugs dropped their muskets and became prisoners, but from where I stood I could see there was one prisoner missing. There was no sign of the bald-headed gorilla and I knew Schwartz had escaped.

I stumbled down the slope to where the wreckers had based their operation for the night and took the lanterns off the two donkeys the thugs had used to try and lure unsuspecting ships onto the Crabart causeway. I patted their rumps and told them to look for Pedro, but being donkeys they walked in the opposite direction with the kind of stubbornness that would have made my Pedro proud. Marlene had done her job well, or possibly the storm had just blown itself out, and by the light of the moon I could see the debris the wreckers had left behind, from half-eaten sandwiches to broken swords. I suddenly felt in need of a weapon and bent down to pick up a discarded knife but I never reached it.

"Secure the wench," snarled Schwartz. "Tie her hands but leave her legs free. She has some walking to do, but not much."

Rough hands seized me round the throat and others pinned my arms to my sides, making sure I had no chance of fighting back. I turned, looked at Schwartz and saw more hatred on his one face than I'd seen in my whole life. And I was its focus.

"Walk, girl. Follow the cliff path and don't expect a rescue because as usual Lewis has gone leaving you to answer for his actions tonight. Walk and don't even consider running away. You can think about flying though." He laughed leaving no doubt what he meant as I made my way slowly up the path towards the Leap of Faith and certain death.

I have to admit I nearly needed a change of underwear, but I had time to wonder why the heck Marlene looked at her PortalVision and decided to help us sort out the weather, but so far hadn't come screaming down to rescue me from Schwartz as he marched me up the cliff path. The bald-headed gorilla kept jabbing me in the back so hard that I nearly fell on the slippery stones, not that he could have cared. I was going to take a far greater fall in a few minutes and for the first time in my life I was truly afraid.

The path stopped climbing and levelled off so that in the moonlight I could see where the cliff curved high above a sweeping cove. Far below, the sea churned on half-exposed rocks even though the storm had calmed to a gentle breeze, turning the foaming spray into a silver mist. Unfortunately, its beauty was lost on me as I was more concerned with wondering whether I could somehow take the Leap of Faith and miss the deadly meat grinder far below.

"Move, wench." Schwartz pushed me forward again and this time I did slip, stunning myself on the rocky path. He made no move to help me beyond giving me a toe poke and my mumbled *I was admiring the view* was a waste of bravado. "Get up, you're nearly there." I had the sudden thought that it would be nice to be called Tertia one last time and not wench, even if it was by Schwarz.

Schwartz tied a short length of rope to my wrists and was now using it to pull me to the cliff edge. I looked down and in spite of what I'd been through on top of Nelson's column my head swam. I'd known I wasn't going to fall off the column but now my feet were already skidding towards the drop on the slippery grass and Schwartz was doing nothing to help me.

"Tell me the truth, girl. Did you tell your friend Gawain I would be operating at the Crabart tonight? Be careful and think before you answer."

I knew what happened to anyone who betrayed Schwartz and I was pretty sure the giant knew I was responsible for the night's disaster, so why was he asking the question? I took a deep breath of defiance. "I told him ... the White Knight, Sir Gawain, Mr Lewis, whatever you want to call him. I did it because he *is* my friend and he trusts me. No other reason."

Schwartz looked at me somewhat surprised and sneered. "Very well, Tertia. For the moment you can live, because for once you've told me the truth. Had you lied, the Leap is always hungry and at this moment you would have been learning to fly, but for now, girl, you're coming with me to my house. For the time being you're my guarantee of a safe passage."

Schwartz pulled me back from the Leap's edge and dragged me none too gently onto the path. The man may have been a knight back at Camelot but he was certainly no gentleman.

The path led inland and though I remembered some of it from the morning walk, in moonlight it looked different and was certainly far muddier after the rain. Schwartz walked quickly, avoiding open ground where possible and watching furtively for any movements that could mean pursuers, but there was no one and I half suspected Lewis didn't yet know he hadn't captured their leader when the rest of the wreckers surrendered.

Ahead, I could see the house where even part of the treasure hoard could buy a small country and keep

Schwartz in comfort for the rest of his life, wherever and whenever he chose to go. All he had to do was fill up a couple of bags with his rarest jewels and disappear through the Time Portal, spinning the dials just as I'd once done in Bryn's cellar. We walked under the archway entrance to the courtyard and Schwartz showed no surprise that the place was empty except for two of his bodyguards. He stared at me and if there was a look of sorrow on his face it was fleeting. The two thugs looked at their leader expectantly.

"Dispose of this human trash then lie low for the rest of the night and we'll do a reckoning in the morning." He turned to me. "Goodbye, Tertia, we'll not meet again." Having used my name for the last time he walked into his fortress and it was only then it occurred to me that Neets and Bryn were probably still inside and that Schwartz was in no mood to be hospitable.

The two men drew their knives and advanced on me and I knew for the second time that night I was probably about to die. Once again I decided I'd rather not, but I wasn't sure whether to stand my ground or try to make a run for it. My hands were tied in front of me, which at least made movement easier, though I had an armed man approaching me from either side, which limited my options.

"Come on, girl, make it easy on yourself," said the first thug, though I was pretty sure he really meant me to make it easy for him. As if!

"Don't struggle and it'll all be over before you know it," the second one added.

As they spoke the two men circled me looking for the moment to strike that would cost them the least effort and risk. The first one thrust his knife forward and the second lunged intending to stab me in the back as I threw myself to one side and rolled out of the way across the cobbles. I was quick, but even so I felt the knife cut into my robe before nicking my shoulder blade, and the pain stung badly. I was still alive, but as I tried to get up one of the thugs put a foot on my neck and laughed as I struggled to move.

"Have it your own way, girl." The other man pricked me on the throat with the point of his blade and drew it slowly back for the kill. He grinned in anticipation, then slumped forward and lay still.

I felt the foot leave my neck and a second body sprawl unconscious across my legs making any thought of running away impossible. I managed to turn my neck and raise my head enough to recognise the person standing next to the pile of bodies.

"Hallo, Miss Jones, it's nice to see you." I managed to shuffle out from under one of the bodies so I could sit up. "Out on a night-time nature walk with the whole school?"

"None of your cheek, young Tertia," There was a chuckle in Miss Jones's voice. "I came looking for my new teaching assistant, and it seems I was right that you need my help. And yes, as you suggested earlier today, I did bring the whole school." Miss Jones's children stood grinning and held onto a lethal collection of catapults and slingshots. "Now stand up and let's get those ropes off your wrists."

I did as I was told and massaged the circulation back into my hands. "It's great to see you all, but it's Bryn and Neets that are going to need help more than me. They're in the house looking round like a couple of tourists and Schwartz has gone down to his cellar to grab a bag of treasure. We've got to look for them before he breaks up a promising friendship.

Miss Jones had been a teacher for long enough to recognise the signs. "I take it young Unita rather likes our Bryn? I'm his aunt so you can tell me."

I shuffled my feet and blushed, because I was sure that the last person Bryn would want to tell was his aunt, but then she was also the nearest thing he had to a mother.

"Nothing wrong with that," said Miss Jones sensing the obvious. "Now, tell me what's been going on."

The night's events may have taken a couple of hours to unfold, but it took me less than five minutes to update Miss Jones. It would have been quicker, but the kids wanted every detail and for a few minutes I was back teaching history and geography.

"We'll look after these two," said the head teacher nodding towards the would-be murderers who were both groaning and clutching their heads, "and then if you don't mind we'll go and help Mr Lewis. If you need us, of course, then give a call and we'll come running."

The two thugs were expertly tied up and left in the yard to nurse aching heads, though their greatest worry should have been explaining to Schwartz how a girl had escaped, how a bunch of kids had defeated two armed men and, most important, why they should avoid taking the Leap of Faith.

I ran into the house and was fairly certain where to look first as I sprinted into the dining hall and came to a skidding halt. On one of the tables, looking like an old discarded rat was Schwartz's wig, though its owner was nowhere to be seen. The secret door to the underground treasure caves was wide open and without a thought I raced down the stone steps not knowing what I was likely to find.

Who am I kidding? Yes I did. I knew I'd find two good friends and one really angry wrecker intent on murder.

Chapter Eleven

The Salt House Manacles and a Race
Against Time and Tide

I'd always expected the air in the cellars to be musty, so was surprised yet again how pleasantly warm it was and how fresh it smelled. There was even the tang of sea salt in the background reminding me of a newly opened bag of crisps.

The door to Schwartz's treasure room was open and I could hear the muffled voices of my two friends talking excitedly about what sounded like jewels.

Probably rings, but then I'm such a young cynic. I ran across, ready to shout a warning that the wrecker was somewhere in the house when a hand clamped over my mouth and an arm went round my throat.

"Don't make a sound, girl," the wrecker growled. "I've got to hand it to you, you're good, but you're not good enough. You've escaped death twice tonight but there won't be a third time. Now move forward slowly, I want to see what the other two brats have been doing." I inched forward in the dim lantern light coming from the treasure room, ready to be choked if I gave any warning of our presence.

Bryn at least had no idea we were there and was too busy exploring to have noticed. "Unita, there's an entrance over there." He raised his lantern, letting the light shine on a large wooden door that, as I knew only too well, hid some of Schwartz's most treasured items. "Keep watch for me while I go and check it out."

Bryn crept inside the new room and whistled, which was something he hardly ever did, and when Neets joined him she was speechless, which was something equally rare. Schwartz and I watched as the light from their lanterns glittered off the carefully displayed hoard of jewels, as well as highlighting the ornaments and paintings, and it didn't take too much imagination to realise that someone knew their value and probably even respected it.

"Schwartz?" Neets said in surprise.

"Must be, I suppose, though I wouldn't have put him down as an art lover."

Neets opened another door at the far end of the room and stepped into an even larger area full of life-size models wearing the most beautiful clothes I'd ever seen. Our shopping trips into history with Marlene hadn't prepared Neets for this.

"Dolce and Gabbana!" she breathed. "One of these dresses and a few of the sparklers from out there and Tertia and I would be... Ladies!"

Bryn was less impressed and becoming aware of their danger. "We've found what we came for so let's get out of here and ask my dad's men to take charge of this stuff."

Neets reluctantly followed him into the first display room and noticed the eggcup standing on the marble and mahogany plinth. "I bet that must be worth something, Bryn. It's got its own display and everything. Wonder what it's for?"

"For a diamond the size of an egg," growled a voice behind them. Schwartz pushed me forward so that I bumped into Bryn. This time the *click* was of two pistols being cocked as his aim covered the three of us. I guessed he probably had spares and a sharp sword as a backup. We raised our hands. "Turn round slowly and face me."

We did as we were told and faced our old enemy from Camelot. The giant was unmistakable even without his wig and just looked a few years older and a lot nastier.

"Typical. Always crops up like a bad penny," I said massaging my throat and giving several tuts. "Just when you think you've got rid of him, there he is right as rain and twice as wet."

"Probably not the time for backchat, Tersh." Neets was quite right, but I do like a show of bravado. "I doubt if he's in any mood to be nice, all things considered."

"Wise words." Schwartz waved one of the pistols at the door then pointed at Bryn. "You, boy. Right now I don't care about you. Get outside and if you can get past my two men go and join your father. I'll come for you both later." Bryn was given no option but to leave as he ran up the stairs into the house. There was no doubt the alternative was to be shot and that wouldn't have been of help to anyone. Schwartz pointed his pistols at Neets and me. "You two walk ahead and no tricks."

In the outer cavern Neets went to climb the steps leading to the house, but Schwartz laughed. "Not up there, keep going and I'll tell you when to stop. I have a little surprise for you both. As a reward for all you've done to me both here and in Camelot I'm going to give you a room to yourselves, though you'll find it has a touch of rising damp."

I had a horrible feeling I knew what he was talking about and in my mind's eye I could see two sets of manacles and a rather wet cave. The walk along the tunnel seemed to take ages, though we had the advantage over Schwartz that we didn't need to crouch too much even near the end when the roof became rock and dropped by more than a foot.

"Careful going down the steps," said Schwartz. "I wouldn't want you to slip and hurt yourselves." Most considerate, I thought.

At the bottom we stood in a cave I remembered only too well, and it wasn't just the cold and damp that made me shiver. The walls were wet and dripping with slime, while the floor was already two to three inches deep in rapidly rising water. One end of the cave was completely bricked up, though near the floor a couple of bricks had been knocked out to let in the seawater.

"Where are we, Tersh?"

"Down at sea level and from the distance we walked probably not too far from Port Eynon. Probably in a cave and not one we're going to like too much."

"Very good!" Schwartz put down his lantern and gave a mocking round of applause, although he still managed to keep his pistols aimed at us. "Now get over to that wall." He pointed at me. "You, put those manacles on your friend's wrists. If you hesitate, I'll shoot her." I did as I was told. "Now put one of your wrists in the other manacle." I did so and Schwartz carefully secured my other wrist giving me no chance to struggle, let alone escape because each set of manacles was linked by a chain that ran through a ring fastened to the wall. Neets and I could move our arms, but that was small comfort.

"I suppose you're going to keep us down here as hostages with only bread and water," said Neets, almost hopefully. "Our friends will come looking and when they find us they'll go looking for you."

"I'm sure you're right," said Schwartz as he walked back to the steps. "But by that time you'll be learning to hold your breath under water." The tide had risen at least another three inches and was up to our kneecaps. "And finding you can't."

"Just water then," I muttered, "no bread."

"My Bryn will find us," Neets said defiantly, "and when he does you'll be sorry!"

"You and the boy, is it?" Schwartz smiled. "Well I'm sorry to have to tell you that he will have met with two of my men and is probably examining his own insides by now. Sorry."

I was impressed for two reasons. Firstly because Neets didn't burst into tears and secondly because she used a string of words that were seriously not ladylike and sounded like they could be worth looking up. It also occurred to me that Schwartz hadn't actually said that Bryn was dead and a man like that would have gloated instead of just hinting. Besides, I knew the two men were trussed up like turkeys. I gave Neets a reassuring wink.

"Sorry, Neets," I said, "I was wrong. We're not at

sea level, we're under it. I think this is the bottom of the Salt House and the tide's got a few more feet to come."

"Quite right," said Schwartz, "and now I must be going. I'll even leave you a lantern so you can see the water level rising." He climbed the steps and disappeared along the tunnel. There was no gloating and no clever witty repartee. He just went.

"You reckon he's really going to let us drown, Tersh?"

"That man was going to destroy Camelot, plus he's wrecked countless ships and drowned their crews. I really don't think he'd give a second thought about getting rid of us, so it's a good job I'm a clever little detective. I nicked this from one of Schwartz's treasure store rooms." I had a small jewelled knife in my hand that was probably worth a large fortune and began to gouge away at the rock around my manacle ring. The knife cut in deeply enough so that I reckoned I'd be able to free myself and then free Neets. Around three weeks would do it, but I wasn't going to tell my cousin.

The tide rose to our waists and showed no sign of stopping. Time and Tide ... as the saying goes, and it was bloody cold.

"Tersh?" Neets's voice trembled and she sounded like I felt. "I'm taller than you."

Not quite what I expected her to say, but I got her meaning. I was going to go under before her. "Yes, but you're heavier than me, so I'll float as long as you can stand on tiptoe." We both giggled because being on the point of dying can do that to you and I should know because I'd been there three times in the past hour.

"Tersh, do you think Bryn managed to get away?"

"I know he did, kid. That boy of yours is quite a lad. In fact I'm banking on him escaping, because he's just about the only hope we've got of getting out of this mess."

"What, you think he'll double back down the tunnel and rescue us?"

"I hope not. He'll only run into Schwartz and the bastard'll kill him out of hand. No, I'm hoping he's got a good memory and a bit of common sense." The seawater was chest high now. "Within the next few minutes preferably."

I was beginning to feel numb as the cold ate into my limbs and I wasn't sure if I could feel my legs anymore or not. They still seemed to be supporting me and for the time being that was a bonus. As the water crept higher I started wondering whether the Leap of Faith with its two-second drop into certain death might have been the better bet, but I decided there wasn't any such thing as an easier way to die. I was having too much fun as a living detective to become a dead loss.

"Give us a song, Neets."

"What? We're about to drown and you want a

song?"

"Yep. And the louder the better!" There was method in my madness. "Let's give them a couple of verses of the *Wizard's Song*. The naughty version."

"You're going mad, Tersh. Give who, anyway?"

"The people who are coming to rescue us. I would think they're about fifteen to twenty feet away by now, so a good singsong will tell them where we are and that our spirits are still high. Either that, or we've gone completely mad. Ready now? One, two, one, two, three, four. SING!"

I launched into one of Camelot's favourite songs giving it everything I could, and when I came to the naughty words of the *Wizard's Song* I screamed them at the top of my voice. Neets joined me on the second line until the small cave vibrated with our voices. The problem was that I reckoned two more verses and the water would be up to our chins and I was already standing on my toes trying to keep the lapping sea out of my mouth.

We finished the first verse and listened. As I spat out salt water I was sure I could hear what could have been voices, but it could just as easily have been the sea gurgling through the Salt House puddling chamber, or even the cry of a distant seagull. I wasn't giving up yet and I could see Neets mouthing what looked like *come on, Bryn*. It takes a lot to beat a Merl's Girl.

Verse two.

Even Neets was having difficulty keeping the seawater out of her mouth, but we still managed to shout at the right points and gurgle at the rest, but as we finished the last line I knew verse three was going to have to wait for another day, or maybe another lifetime. Then...

Ting! Ting!

"Tersh, did you hear that?"

I gurgled that I had.

Ting! Ting! Clang! Clunk!

"We're in here," Neets shouted alone, because I was now having to breathe through my nose as everything else was below the surface of the rising waters. "Hurry!" A bit unnecessary under the circumstances, I thought. Whoever was outside was hardly going for a tea break.

The sound of hammer blows against the brick wall was getting louder and more urgent and the voices were definitely not seagulls anymore. Even better, the shouts included our names. Mortar dust began to drift into the cave and then I tried to cheer as a brick slid out of the wall and dropped into the water, but my mouth filled with sea and I knew I only had seconds left. A second brick fell and then a third as I started choking on the salty water, then I heard someone shout and felt hands holding my head above the surface so I could cough out a lungful of brine.

"Bryn, see to Unita," shouted Lewis. "I'll free Tertia."

190

I felt the manacles round my wrists loosen and then come away from the wall, but any strength I had in my arms and legs had gone and I flopped forward, drifting into Lewis's arms. I managed to glance across at Neets and saw that Bryn had freed her and was carrying my cousin to the hole in the brick wall made by his father and him. I couldn't help feeling Neets was making the most of things and to my mind clinging a little bit too tightly to Bryn, though he didn't seem to be complaining. Lewis was my White Knight in shining armour as he carried me through the hole in the wall and into the puddling room. I'd stopped coughing and was into the spluttering stage as he took me up the stairs and into the cool night air. I lay on the grass next to Neets and looked at stars I'd never thought I'd see again, then I looked at my cousin. Bryn was kneeling cradling Neets's head in his lap and looking stupidly happy, while Neets just looked happily stupid.

"You okay, kid?"

I got a grin and a wink in reply. "I knew my Bryn would rescue us, Tersh."

"Mmm, for a lad he's not half bad. Mind you considering our only hope was that he'd remember the stories he told us about this place and what we told him about the guided tour Schwartz gave us." I paused. "He may have realised where we were, but I had no idea whether he'd get to us in time."

Bryn looked sheepish and to his credit admitted

that when he left the house he ran into Miss Jones and the schoolchildren and told her what had happened in the cellars. It was when Miss Jones told him she couldn't afford to lose such a good teacher that Bryn realised the only place Schwartz could have taken us was through the tunnel to the Salt House. Knowing that if they went back to the cellars he'd only run into Schwartz, he ran to meet his father and rode to the Salt House racing against the tide.

It had almost been a dead heat.

I could have lain where I was all night. I didn't mind that the grass was soaking wet, because so was I and I was even beginning to feel calm. Weird! When I did move to get up it wasn't through any sense of duty, it was a rasping tongue like wet sandpaper slobbering all over my face. I tried to squirm away but Pedro was very persistent. Neets may have had her Bryn, but I had my donkey. Lewis helped me to my feet and Pedro helped me stay upright when I draped my arms round his neck.

"We brought Pedro and your piebald horse, Unita, because I want the two of you to go home in comfort." Lewis mounted his white stallion and was definitely not aiming in the direction of Port Eynon. Bryn reluctantly released Neets and started to follow his dad.

"Where are you two off to?" There was an edge to Neets's voice.

"To find and stop Schwartz." Lewis wheeled his

192

horse to face us. "Now he's lost pretty well everything he's going to be ten times more dangerous."

"And you thought you'd go off without Tersh and me? You thought you'd send the two girlies back home for a nice cup of tea and a warm bath while you do the man's work? Think again. We're coming with you."

Bryn looked at Neets and with the sort of common sense that said that one day he might just make a good husband, he kept his mouth shut.

"Very well, but we need to ride fast or we'll lose the initiative," Lewis said after what seemed like a long pause, "and I really don't have time to argue, so get mounted and keep up with me. Bryn, get Unita on her horse now." I'd already climbed onto Pedro's back and without wasting further words Lewis spurred his horse into a fast walk. We followed as best we could.

I'd cheated death and Schwartz three times in the past few hours and there was no way I was going to tempt a fourth. I was staying with Lewis from now on. After all, he was my White Knight.

Chapter Twelve

Death of a Knight and
Some Explanations

We arrived at the cliff overlooking the Crabart to find that the wreckers, or at least those that had surrendered, were sitting on the ground tied up hand and foot, while the Redcoat captain and his men guarded them with their muskets cocked. Any small groups that tried to escape had been overcome without much of a struggle and brought back to join the rest of the thugs.

"He's definitely not with this lot," said Lewis after

making a quick check. "I'd hoped he may have put on a wig and be hiding here. He could be anywhere by now."

"We could start looking at his house." I reckoned any suggestion was better than none at all. "We know he went back there after leaving Neets and me in the cave."

"It's not a bad idea," said Lewis, "though I doubt he'll still be there. He'll have grabbed what he could and made a run for it. Blast it! He may even have used his Time Portal. He could be centuries away by now with a small hoard of treasure and a new identity. The only thing we know for sure is that he hasn't been able to go back to Camelot. Merlin saw to that."

It took us less than ten minutes to get to Schwartz's house and though we saw the odd wrecker, they stayed well out of our way and were mostly trying to avoid being caught by Redcoat soldiers. Even the courtyard was deserted with the exception of two thugs, trussed hand and foot and pretending to be unconscious. After what they'd put me through I was tempted to give them a good kicking, but as we got nearer I noticed each of them had a dark red stain on his chest. They weren't unconscious and Schwartz had taken his revenge for their failure.

There wasn't a sign of anyone in the building and the only sounds were the creepy ones you might get at night in any old house. We searched all the rooms looking for some sort of clue as to where Schwartz might have gone, but there was nothing and eventually we ended up in the main dining hall. The dying embers of the fire gave out enough warmth for us to be grateful, but not enough to dry our clothes; however it did keep us quiet for a few moments, which was enough for me to hear the muffled tapping.

I put my ear to the wooden panel hiding the stone steps leading to Schwartz's treasure caves. "Quiet." I held up my hand. "There's someone in the secret passage." I started to pull the lever that opened the hidden door.

Lewis drew his sword. "Careful, Tertia, it could be Schwartz. I'll cover you." He was obviously prepared to skewer anyone who came out, but luckily he lowered his sword just in time as the crush of cheering kids rushed into the room while Miss Jones followed more sedately brushing dust off her dress. I looked behind her into the passage, but there was no sign of Schwartz.

"He locked us in there, the pig," said the head teacher. "While we were looking around his cellars he came out of a tunnel and nearly knocked me over, though to be honest, I think he was more surprised than me. He kept trying to get to a colourful machine in the corner, but my children let fly with their catapults and he ran up the stairs snarling like an animal." Miss Jones looked proudly at the kids and so did I, because I reckoned they were mine too. "We tried to follow him, but he shut the door and locked us in here. I take it he's gone?"

"He's gone, yes," said Lewis, "but not before he murdered his two men in the courtyard."

"I'm sorry for that," said Mrs Jones. "We tied them up after they tried to kill Tertia, but maybe killing helpless people is the level Schwartz has fallen to."

"He never rose above it, my dear," said Lewis. "Never." I knew he was thinking about his wife as well as all the harm the man had done in Camelot as the Black Knight. "However, at least we know now he didn't use his Time Portal to escape so he can't be too far away. There's still a chance we can catch him before the night's out."

"So what are we doing standing here chatting?" I was all for action. "I want that man. He's tried to kill me three times here as well as once on the church tower and it's a habit I want to stop." Neets and Bryn were already half way through the door to the courtyard; after all Schwartz had killed Bryn's mother, though I thought it best not to point out to Neets that the man had also brought her and Bryn together, so to speak.

Those of us who had horses, or in my case a Pedro, mounted up and trotted towards the headland coast path, while Miss Jones and the kids followed close behind. The moon was now full and high, giving everything a clear silvery colour that made our ride so much easier than the walk to Schwartz's house had been earlier. When we reached the path and dismounted I realised with a shudder that we were standing at the Leap of Faith, where on a whim Schwartz had let me live. Below us the sea still churned around the rocks and the white spray flew, even though the storm had gone and it still meant almost certain death.

Something caught my eye and I looked along the cliff path towards the Worm's Head. The wrecker was silhouetted in the moonlight, dark, evil and no more than a hundred yards away.

Schwartz was so preoccupied with his thoughts that he didn't see us blocking his path until it was too late. Lewis stared at his enemy and his smile was ice cold as he motioned the rest of us to back away, because this was his fight and ours to watch. There was no question of surrender on either side and the two men didn't waste time on words with so many years of history fuelling their hatred. They flew at each other snarling and clawing like animals even though they were heavily armed. Schwartz tried to gouge out his old enemy's eyes as Lewis grabbed him round the neck then slammed a fist into Schwartz's face making his nose gush blood. The wrecker hardly seemed to notice as he used his knees, elbows, and head to try to dislodge Lewis, making contact but without effect until one lucky kick made my old friend grimace in pain.

They separated for a moment, circling each other

like a pair of wrestlers, and I saw Schwartz pull out a long knife that had an edge he could have shaved his head with. He crouched low like a professional fighter, passing the knife from hand to hand and feinting lunges so Lewis wouldn't guess how he was going to thrust. He drew the knife back and prepared to strike with all the pent-up venom of a lifetime of hatred. Even I knew he couldn't miss.

Twang. A slingshot stone smacked into Schwartz's arm with the force of a bullet, causing him to drop the knife and howl with unexpected pain.

"Miss Jones!" Lewis's face broke into a grin as the children rushed towards him followed by their teacher. "How did you all get here so quickly?"

Everyone was concentrating on Miss Jones and Lewis, so no one noticed Schwartz pick up his knife until he ran screaming at Lewis with the blade raised ready to kill. Lewis had little chance of escaping Schwartz's attack as he crouched down to make himself as small a target as possible, and the anguished look on Bryn's face told me he knew he was going to lose his father because of the wrecker, just as he had his mother. There was no time to do anything.

A musket shot rang out and I swear I felt the wind from the ball as it flew past my neck before striking Schwartz on the forehead. It only stopped him for a couple of seconds as he gave a shout of fury, but that was enough.

Someone shouted: "Duck!"

The hailstorm of catapult and slingshot stones smashed into every part of Schwartz's body before he could land a blow, making him scream with pain and stagger backwards off the path. A second and third fusillade hit their mark driving him farther towards the cliff edge and Schwartz's look of hatred turned to one of surprise and then of horror as he teetered on the edge of the cliff. His feet slipped out from under him on the loose grass before he slid inch by inch over the precipice, his fingers desperately grabbing at crumbling earth. I stared into Schwartz's eyes and saw nothing but empty hatred as the giant disappeared with a low moan into the dark void. Anyone else would have screamed.

"It's the Leap of Faith," said Bryn. "He's gone over his own Leap of Faith."

"He's gone, Bryn, and that's all that matters," said his father, putting an arm round his son's shoulder. "It's taken eighteen years, but at long last it's over and we can lead normal lives for once. Let's get everyone together and go home."

I looked around to see who had fired such an incredible shot with a weapon as notoriously inaccurate as a musket. There were lots of kids with slings and a few men with pistols, but no one had anything like a musket. Somewhere it looked as though we had a friend who wanted to remain anonymous.

Mrs Jones arrived minutes before us and welcomed

everyone back to the Lewis home with plates of sandwiches, hot sweet tea, and a warming log fire. She was amazing. Whenever she appeared a feast of food seemed to materialise within minutes. Mind you, with her help it always disappeared just as quickly. Inspector Smollett had been dozing in a chair with a blanket over his shoulders, staring into the flames with frequent trips to the window. Now I sat surrounded by some of my adoring school kids as I told them all about my adventures since arriving in Port Eynon and what it had been like being with the wreckers. Neets was surrounded by her adoring Bryn.

After he'd eaten, Lewis told us all again how Schwartz had died while Miss Jones and Mrs Jones proudly related the exploits of the school kids and Mr Lewis's servants. Everyone had a story to tell and no one was bored in the telling, or the hearing.

"From what I gather," said my Inspector Smollett, "Schwartz had a fortune in stolen treasure, most of which he stole using his Time Portal. What's going to happen to that loot?" He was a typical copper.

"The rest of you met my brother-in-law, the Redcoat captain," said Lewis as we nodded. "He and some of his men are busy cataloguing everything, but by the look of things it will be a good many days before they finish. Some of the more valuable items are quite possibly from centuries in the past, or maybe even the future, so we may never be able to return them. However, what we can send back will be taken to the rightful owners, anonymously of course."

I still felt there were a few questions left unanswered. There was Nelson's statue and the Koh-i-noor diamond, as well as the disappearance of Bryn's mother. Then most important, there was the blooming friendship between Bryn and Neets. No, it wasn't over yet.

During the following days I watched over Neets like a mother hen, following her and Bryn from a distance as they walked on the headland and talked. Occasionally they laughed, but mostly they talked. Only later did Neets give me a hint as to what they said.

"It's Marie," she said. "It's his mum. All this good stuff's happened, but he'd give up everything just to be able to see her once."

I was silent for a moment as I swirled the dregs in my teacup before throwing them on the fire. As an apprentice wizard I could sort of read the future in tea leaves far better than Neets, especially if I had a few hints. I tried now, focusing my thoughts on Bryn and let his life fly through my mind like a recorded film. I sped through the images leading up to the present day and then allowed everything to slow down until I found the scene I wanted. Then I stopped. I frowned at what I saw and shook my head to clear out the thoughts, because the future is always a bit fuzzy and nothing's ever certain. In Bryn's case the past was just as blurred, but it was what else I saw that confused me. I faked a smile for Neets's benefit.

"Mmm, his mum," I said, as though I'd known all along. "Yeah, that's what I thought. Look, let me sleep on it, because I don't think things are as they seem, or at least not as we thought they were." I was beginning to act like the older and bossier of the two of us, but then it's often said that boyfriends make your brain wither into mush.

I lay awake thinking about what I'd seen in the tea leaves, worrying why there were still parts of the Schwartz mystery that seemed to be unresolved, if only I could work out which parts they were. Halfway through breakfast the next day I leapt to my feet, spilling porridge and a plate of seaweed in my excitement.

"That's it!" I looked down at the mess on the floor. "Sorry about the carpet. Actually I expect seaweed's quite good for it." I took a breath to calm myself and grinned. "So many things just haven't seemed right up until now, at least to me, but I think I may have worked out one or two. The only place I'll know for sure is up at Schwartz's and if anyone wants to join me I'll explain everything on the way." I spoke the last words as I disappeared through the door at a pace approaching a fast Pedro trot. No one was going to miss out and Lewis was closely followed by Inspector Smollett, Neets, and Bryn as the front door opened and we all streamed into the driveway. I almost broke into a canter down the path leading to the stables.

As we neared the top of the headland, the others turned and waited while Pedro and I caught up at a gentle trot. He may have been a donkey, but he was no fool, because no one was going anywhere without him and me. We grouped up and I took the lead, talking as we went.

"We know why the Black Knight came here and became Schwartz," I said, "and why you followed him, Gawain – sorry, Lewis. It was a complete fluke and you had no choice in the matter. It could have been anywhere and anytime, but spookily Port Eynon in 1716 suited Schwartz and he took to wrecking, smuggling, and terrorism like a duck to water. It wasn't too much different from what he did in Camelot really and he'd be a murderous pig wherever he went, as Neets and I know only too well."

"As do I," said Lewis, "and so does Bryn. However, I'm glad chance brought us here or I wouldn't have met my Marie."

"And I wouldn't be here at all," said Bryn.

"And I … I'm going to say nothing," Neets said wisely, because this was not the time.

The door to Schwartz's manor house was wide open and pretty well everything that was small enough to be moved had either been taken by the Redcoat soldiers or put to better use by enthusiastic locals. Nevertheless, I was sure that somewhere in the building would be what I wanted, I just didn't know what it would be or even what it would look like, but

I couldn't tell anybody that. *You'll know it when you see it,* was the best I could do.

Bryn, Neets, and I started searching the upper floors, but with the exception of a few empty packing cases we found nothing of any interest. The human locusts had already stripped the place. Lewis and Inspector Smollett explored the downstairs rooms and drew a similar blank, although to be honest I hadn't expected anything dramatic. I knew it wouldn't be obvious or someone would already have seen it. Whatever it was would be hidden and probably near where Schwartz had squirrelled away the rest of his treasures.

"You mentioned he had a Time Portal under here somewhere, Tertia," Lewis said and I nodded. "Show me where it is then please, because I really don't think we'll find anything up here. Schwartz is no fool, but then neither am I, and if I was him I'd hide anything I didn't want found where no one had access to it except me."

I led the way into the main dining hall, pulled the lever by the fireplace and with a *click* the panel in the wall slid open. Neets and I found lanterns, lit them and handed them out before leading the way down the steps into Schwartz's secret treasure rooms. The Portal was still humming gently to itself and the dimmest of ultraviolet glows made the outline of an archway just visible.

"I wonder where his other Portal is?" I murmured

as I examined the dials and controls. They were pretty much the same as those on our own device.

"Why? Do you think he had another?" said Lewis. "I only have one and manage to get around quite well enough."

"Oh, for most purposes one Portal is fine, but Marlene tells me that for going short distances in the same time period then two are necessary. Remember how we used to nip around Camelot, Neets? We had two then, but only for local journeys." Neets nodded. "Well, looking at the controls I reckon he used this for really short journeys as well as long ones. And I mean really short."

"You're saying Schwartz had a secret hiding place?"

I nodded as I continued twiddling knobs before standing back with a smile of satisfaction. "Right, I've reset the dials. Any volunteers to be the first to go through?"

Bryn and Lewis nodded as I expected they would and walked without hesitation into the ultraviolet glow and disappeared.

Zzzzzp.

Neets almost ran through closely followed by me and my Inspector Smollett bringing up a more dignified rear.

Zzzzzp.

We were definitely in a cave and what would have been the entrance was completely bricked up with the exception of a small number of holes several feet above ground level. The walls and floor were fairly dry, even though we were in a sea cave and the brickwork had been put there to keep both the water and prying eyes out, while letting fresh air in.

"So this is what Culver Hole looks like from the inside," said Bryn almost in awe. "Ever since I was a kid I've wanted to see in here. So have all my friends, but none of us could find a way in and the outside was always too slippery to climb to the first gap. Even then we wouldn't have been able to see inside because it's too dark."

Lewis touched the bricks, which must have been five-feet thick at least, then turned to me. "And you reckon this was where Schwartz used to go if things got too hot for him? It makes sense. Whenever we got too close for comfort he always managed to disappear until things quieted down."

Neets wasn't so sure. "But anyone could have followed him through the Portal under his house and he'd have been caught like a rat in a trap because the dials would have been set for here."

"Not necessarily," I said. "Remember how I went back to change the dials on the Portal in Lewis's cellar when I brought Bryn to the *Olé Grill* restaurant? I just put my arm through the one in our cave and changed the dials on Mr Lewis's. I would imagine Schwartz did the same sort of thing. Not only that, but there would have been nothing to have stopped him going anywhere by using *this* Portal. I doubt if he

207

stayed here much."

"But you just brought us here so he can't have switched the dials, Tersh." Sometimes my cousin can be infuriatingly logical.

"That's what makes me think he didn't use it much, and then only as a place he knew he wouldn't be disturbed. I don't think he hid here." I scanned the contents of the cave with a look of distaste. "Comfortable isn't the word that springs to mind."

In one corner was a leather armchair and footstool, while in the centre of the cave stood a small wooden dining table and one chair. A log fire was surrounded by a ring of stones, but most interesting of all, at least to me, was an antique writing desk that actually looked as though the owner cared for it.

As I walked across the cave I touched one of the logs on the fire, but it was stone cold and the grey embers crumbled to dust, so I knew the wrecker hadn't been here for a day or two at least. I opened the largest of the desk's drawers and took out a thick leather-bound book and a much slimmer one that looked the more used. I quickly thumbed through the bigger of the two to make sure it was what I'd expected, then did the same with the smaller one and grinned.

"Okay," said Lewis with just a tinge of impatience, "What's all this about, Tertia? Why are two books so interesting?"

208

"It occurred to me that a man who stole valuable works of art and displayed them for his personal pleasure so carefully was probably going to catalogue things." I held up the large book. "If I'm right this will tell us everything Schwartz stole since he came to Port Eynon and where he stole it from. That'll make your Redcoat captain's job a bit easier. It also occurred to me that if the wrecker did that then he'd probably keep a journal of some sort. I know it was a bit of a chance, but I was right." I held up the slimmer book."With any luck it'll tell us the one thing we all want to know. What really happened to Marie ... to Bryn's mum."

"He killed her," said Bryn with venom. He tried to grab the book, but I managed to dodge. "He killed my mum and boasted about it."

"Possibly," I said, "though I'd like to know the truth and hopefully it's going to be in here. Not even Schwartz would lie in his diary. It'd be pointless." I started walking towards the Portal. "Anyway it's chilly down here, so let's go back to your house, Bryn, and warm up. I have a little story to tell you and it's not the one I thought it was." I gave a wry little smile. "Well not exactly anyway. Let's go."

I reset the dials on the Portal and watched four bemused people walk into the ultraviolet archway.

Zzzzzp, Zzzzzp, Zzzzzp, Zzzzzp.

I changed the setting and followed them, though I had a little detour I wanted to make it to the *Olé Grill* for a chat with Marlene before meeting up with my friends in Lewis's mansion.

Zzzzzp.

Chapter Thirteen

A Bad Penny, Limbo
and a Welcome Return

When I got back to Port Eynon everyone was sitting in Mrs Jones's kitchen while the housekeeper started preparing food. None of us was hungry, but old habits die hard and after all lunch is lunch. I sat down, placing the two books on the table in front of me and looked at my friends, but nobody said a thing. They didn't even ask me why I came through the Portal a minute or two after them. I picked up the big book and dropped it on the table with a bang.

"Okay," I said at last, "as I mentioned before, the first book is a list of all the incredibly valuable works of art Schwartz stole and though it's amazing in itself, it wasn't what I was really looking for. The other book told me what I wanted to know and a lot more besides."

"And if we wait around long enough," said Lewis with just a trace of impatience, "maybe you'll tell us what *we* want to know."

"I doubt it," said Smollett. "She'll get to the *and the murderer is* bit and someone'll shout—"

"Lunch!" Mrs Jones started clattering dinner plates onto the table and I quickly gathered up the books. "It's a buffet so you can help yourselves and eat while Tertia tells her story." As she spoke, she grabbed a number of chicken legs, several thick slices of ham and beef, a hunk of cheese and pickle, three boiled eggs and a doorstep of homemade bread thick with butter. "No pudding for me. I'm trying to lose a bit of weight." She laughed for the sheer joy of eating, while the rest of us helped ourselves to what was left.

With a sandwich in each hand I told them what I'd discovered in Schwartz's journal. "Back in Camelot the White Knight – that's you Mr Gawain Lewis – defeated the Black Knight and took him to Arthur's castle."

"I still have his black helmet tucked away somewhere as a keepsake," said Lewis.

"We know," said Neets. "We found it and that's

what made us think you were the Black Knight."

"Anyway, you both came to Port Eynon through Merlin's one-way-only portable Portals around eighteen years ago, although Schwartz got here a year earlier and by the time you arrived he was already established as the chief wrecker and local bad guy. He had little choice but to stay, because you knew his secret. You knew he travelled in Time and most important you also married the woman he loved, but who rejected him." There was a gasp from Mrs Jones and Lewis laid a comforting hand on her arm. Bryn said nothing but looked grim. "He didn't dare leave here in case you invaded his fortress and found his treasures and his Portal. He had to stay."

"You're saying Schwartz loved my mum?" Bryn said in protest. "He couldn't have, he had her killed." Neets nodded vigorously in agreement.

"I know it's amazing," I said, "but this book is definite about it. He saw her riding by on the headland many times and always noted it down. But every time he tried to talk to her she spurred her horse and rode away. The notes in his diary turn from interest, to desire, then to love, but when Marie rejected him he probably decided that if he couldn't have her then neither would his deadliest enemy."

"There's nothing new there," said Lewis. "We've always known Schwartz killed my wife."

"Really?" I said, "How do we know? As far as I can make out no one has ever heard Schwartz say he killed

Marie. In fact to me it always sounded as though he regretted her disappearance and that's why I wanted to read his journal if it existed."

"And what does the book say?" said my inspector Smollett. "He probably lied in it so there'd be no evidence."

"Like I said, people don't lie in private journals, especially when the book's hidden in a cave with no way in. Anyway let me read what he wrote the night that Marie vanished." I cleared my throat and opened the slim book at a marked page.

"I have often wished to kill Lewis (I can't think of him as Gawain the White Knight now Camelot is finished) for taking away the only woman I ever loved; indeed the only person I had any feelings for. Tonight she was taken from both of us so that neither shall see her again in this life. Those of my men who caused her horse to bolt have taken the Leap of Faith, while I spared those that tried to stop her horse going over the cliffs into the sea far below. I managed to open the Portal as her horse leapt and though she disappeared through the archway I have no way of knowing whether she fell to her death or whether I saved her. I will however take great pleasure in watching the pain in Lewis's face when he finds out Marie is gone and hope the hurt he will suffer in the years to come will be no less than mine. He will assume I killed her and I will let him think so to make his pain the greater."

I closed the book. "I don't think he killed Marie. In fact I'm not even sure now that she's dead. I'm not saying she's definitely still alive, but it would seem possible."

Bryn stared at me open-mouthed and Lewis did the same.

"She can't be alive." Bryn said it so quietly that I had to lean forward to hear him. "There were witnesses. People saw her go over the Leap of Faith on her horse."

"Yes they did," I said, "but they expected her to go crashing onto the rocks below, so that's what their minds told them actually happened. In fact, it looks as though Schwartz saved, rather than killed her, by opening up his Portal. The trouble is, if that's the case we can't be sure where he sent her and now he's gone, even the wrecker himself can't tell us."

"Does he say anything else?" Lewis looked like a man whose last hope was being dangled just beyond his reach.

"Not about Marie, but he does write about me and Neets. He calls us *the two little wenches from Camelot* and I don't think he liked us very much. He tells how he spotted us outside your house and then tried to kill me in the church – well done Mr Inspector Smollett – then saw us again when we walked out of Bryn's house and he realised we'd found Lewis's Portal. The *little wenches from Camelot* were hot on his trail.

Incidentally it was him that Bryn and I saw coming into the cellar when Bryn first went into the business of statue transportation. Schwartz wanted to wreck the Portal before I could use it but he was just a little bit too late."

"My Marie may be alive," said Lewis, echoing his son.

"Yes. There's not much we can do about it yet, though I did take the journal to Marlene and got her opinion and she had one or two ideas. I tell you, reading through his journal was like a *Who's Who of Extreme Nastiness*."

"About the only thing he didn't do was steal the crown jewels," said Smollett.

"Only because I beat him to it." Lewis smiled grimly.

"He knew who did it too," said Bryn, "and that was another reason for him to hate you, Dad. You not only married Mum, but you stopped him stealing the diamond."

Lewis bit into a hunk of bread and cheese. "In his eyes he had good reason to hate me then."

Neets was looking thoughtful, which usually meant someone was in for a barbed comment. This time though she was only being thoughtful. "Tersh, if we know everything Schwartz did and all the terrible events that happened because of him, why don't we use the Time Portal to go back and stop him doing them?"

216

"Because you know it doesn't work that way, Neets. Think about it. If things have already happened then history will always find some other way of making them still take place even if we go back and change things. You can make history happen and sort of complete it, like Lewis did with the diamond, but you can't change it."

"He still took my Marie from me," said Lewis.

"Yes, he did that," I said quietly, "but what's done can't be undone and life goes on for all of us. Schwartz is finished and it's an ending." I sounded so grown up.

Mrs Jones released Lewis's hand and cleared away the dishes. Like it or not, I thought, it really was an ending and the start of a new chapter. We all had our memories and for some, like Bryn and Neets, I suspected the future had a wealth of experiences in store and for others the nightmares of the past years would fade, becoming half-remembered dreams.

It was an ending of sorts.

The next two days were sunny and very warm as though the weather was trying to make up for the storms of the previous week. Miss Jones and I took the kids on walks over the dunes and I found out just how much I knew about nature from my days with Merlin, as well as how much fun it was to pass that knowledge on. We investigated the Salt House and Schwartz's lair, discovering a number of hidden passages and tunnels that seemed to lead nowhere except back on themselves. The kids thought it was marvellous and spent almost half a day playing hide-and-seek.

I was very careful to avoid the subject of time travel and Time Portals. It would only have caused problem questions, not the least of which would have been *Where's Camelot, Miss?* and *Does that mean you could be Bryn's great, great, great granny, Miss?* Questions best avoided.

Lewis kept himself busy as the local magistrate, presiding over the court hearings of those wreckers either not thought to be ringleaders, or just too stupid to have resisted Schwartz's promises of wealth. One by one their names and crimes were read out and those who showed genuine remorse were excused the fate of Swansea castle prison and allowed to serve the community with room and food as their only payment. Mrs Jones's shrewd advice behind the scenes helped many a farm get its harvest in on time thanks to the extra unpaid labour that became available.

Only my Inspector Smollett seemed less than happy. He moped around as though waiting for something to happen when he looked as though he should have been aimlessly skimming stones. The food was good, he slept in a comfortable bed, and his time was his own. To cap it all he told us the weather was better than on any holiday he'd taken in his entire life and Marlene had promised to send him back home in time for the Sunday lunch he thought he'd missed. Yet something was on his mind.

Then the world fell apart.

After dinner on the third evening, Neets and David, the scullery boy, went to the kitchen to make everyone a cup of tea. It was more than half an hour later that I went to see what was keeping them, and it was ten minutes after that when Bryn joined us.

Schwartz was standing at the far end of the room with an arm round Neets's neck and a knife at her throat. He motioned Bryn to sit on the floor next to David and me and put a finger to his lips for silence. His face was covered in blood from a score of cuts and scratches and what was left of his clothes hung off him in tatters. He was a broken mess.

"It's your father I want, boy," he rasped, his normal strong voice sounding like sandpaper, but it had lost none of its chilling menace. "But one false move and I'll happily start with the girl."

Neets knew better than to wriggle and I could see she had no wish to give Schwartz the satisfaction of seeing she was afraid. "We saw you go over the cliff," she said throatily. "You died. How can you be here?"

"Because I want to live," hissed Schwartz, "because I want revenge, because I'm strong and because I was born lucky."

"But you said nobody's ever survived the Leap of Faith." Bryn obviously wanted the giant to talk rather than concentrate on Neets's neck.

"Nor have they, but until now anyone taking the

Leap has done so very reluctantly and been thrown away from the cliff. I slid down the rock face and slowed myself by grabbing outcrops before I hit the water." His hands were swollen and covered in cuts. "I missed the rocks and swam with only one purpose. To get here." He paused. "It sounds like the rest of your little band is about to join us."

"Are you having problems with the kettle, dear," called out Mrs Jones as she opened the kitchen door and walked in followed by Lewis. "Ah, it's you, Mr Wrecker. Tertia said you were a bad penny."

"You don't seem surprised," said Schwartz, making sure everyone saw the knife at Neets's throat.

"To be honest," replied Lewis, "I'm not. You've escaped from me and from the executioner in Camelot. You've made life a misery for this area and murdered sailors without thought. Somehow I couldn't see you being killed by a slingshot and a fall into the sea."

Schwartz laughed, though it sounded more like pebbles being spun in a bowl.

"Let Unita go," said Lewis, trying to move to one side of the wrecker. "She's nothing to you."

"You're going to tell me it's you I want, aren't you. You really are so noble it hurts, Gawain ... sorry, I mean Lewis. Unfortunately you're wrong. I have to admit revenge would be good, but all I want from you right now is the use of your Time Portal. I have a hankering to go back to my house and collect some

220

things, so now you're all here if you wouldn't mind walking ahead of me to the cellar, I'll be gone."

Lewis had no option as he led our small procession down the cellar steps. Schwartz brought up the rear holding the knife to Neets's throat and it took the combined persuasion of Smollett and me to stop Bryn launching himself at the wrecker. We both knew Schwartz wouldn't hesitate to kill Neets.

The Time Portal was still humming gently in the last cellar room and I couldn't help thinking it was a good job these prototype things were built to last, given the amount of use it was getting. Schwartz motioned for everyone to line up against the room's far wall as he dragged Neets towards the shimmering archway and set the dials.

"Don't try to stop me and certainly don't follow. If you try you know I won't hesitate to cut her throat."

Before even Bryn could protest, Neets kicked with her heel catching Schwartz on the kneecap. He bent over with pain and for a second loosened his hold on Neets enough for her to bite the wrecker's wrist and wriggle free. As she ran to Bryn, Schwartz disappeared through the ultraviolet archway leaving a dazed Neets nursing her neck.

Zzzzzp.

I grabbed Lewis by the arm and dragged him to the Portal, almost throwing him through it. "Quick, we have to follow him. I don't care what he said, but I think I know what happens next and it's between you and Schwartz as it always was."

Zzzzzp.

Schwartz was waiting in the main dining hall of his house, leaning against the mantelpiece and sipping a glass of wine. He still looked a mess, but like Lewis he had a charisma of sorts, though the wrecker encouraged obedience by fear rather than respect and trust.

"You came after me then?" said Schwartz almost nonchalantly. "You couldn't be satisfied with leaving me to face the music with the Redcoats that surround this place now, or I have to admit, possibly escaping through my Portal. You could have become the Lord of the Manor without me around. Mind you, I can't say I'm sorry. I'd rather like to finish you off once and for all. Maybe then I'll be able to carry on here where I left off."

"Schwartz, you always did talk too much, even in Camelot." Lewis drew his sword and walked towards the wrecker whose blade was already in the hand not holding a wine glass.

Schwartz snarled and charged at Lewis, throwing the glass at him as he came. His sword scythed through the air, narrowly missing Lewis's face and the return slash cut into the ex-White Knight's sleeve drawing a thin line of blood. Lewis raised his sword to ward off any further attacks and backed off far enough to be a weapon's length away.

Schwartz punctuated every heavy slash with a

verbal battering. "Everywhere I go," *slash*, "everything I do," *slash*, "you're there," *slash*, "or those two brats," *slash*, "or now your son," *slash*, "always interfering," *slash*. "Don't any of you know when to give in?" *double slash*.

Lewis looked surprisingly calm as he parried Schwartz's angry thrusts and his smile just seemed to infuriate the wrecker making it even easier to anticipate his next move. Though Schwartz shooting Lewis wasn't what we'd expected.

With a bellow of rage Schwartz threw his sword at his enemy and drew a pair of pistols from his belt. He stared along one of the barrels aiming at Lewis's heart. "You know, if I was a gentleman I'd offer you the other pistol and we'd duel to the death. But I'm not a gentleman and you're going to die." As he pulled the trigger a window smashed and the pistol spun out of Schwartz's hand, leaving a bloody mess and three fingers. The wrecker screamed in pain and anger as he ran out of the room into the courtyard, holding his mangled hand to his chest. A cheery face appeared at the window and saluted.

"Sorry for interfering, brother-in-law. Thought I'd just keep a beady eye on things in case that nasty piece of villainy was still around and pulled any gutter tricks. As a gentleman, of course you wouldn't be acquainted with that sort of thing."

"You're a marvel, Captain, and I'm a very lucky man."

"Indeed you are, sir. Indeed you are." The captain saluted again and turned his attention to a new commotion in the courtyard. "By the way, Baldy's just come out of the house if you'd care to join us."

Lewis swore under his breath and we hurried out of the building. We needn't have worried, Schwartz had what remained of his hands in the air and was surrounded by a ring of the captain's Redcoats, each of whom had a loaded and primed musket pointed at Schwartz's head. I wondered again who our unseen musket firing friend had been at the Leap of Faith.

"Give the word, brother-in-law, and he'll be full of more lead than a church roof."

"Tempting, my friend," said Lewis, "however if your men would withdraw and if you could give Schwartz a sword I'll finish this once and for all."

Schwartz looked up in surprise. "And if I beat you you'll let me go? These thugs of yours won't use me as target practice?"

"I give you my word. If you beat me fair and square no one will stop you leaving to go wherever you want."

The Redcoat captain reluctantly tossed Schwartz a sword, resisting the temptation to throw it point first. The wrecker caught it and slashed the air, testing the weapon for weight and I remembered him doing much the same on the church roof with a piece of wood. He watched the soldiers as they retreated out of earshot and, more important, accurate musket shot, before smiling.

"You really are a fool, Gawain, or Lewis … whatever you call yourself here. You should have let your Redcoats finish me off while they had the chance. Now the odds are in my favour again."

"How so?" The point of Lewis's sword hadn't moved away from the wrecker's chest for an instant.

"Because I cheat, while you play by the book and because I always carry three pistols. Oh, I admit I've got to aim and fire with my left hand thanks to your captain, but it still gives me a bit of an advantage. You'll agree?"

Schwartz drew his hidden pistol and once again aimed carefully at Lewis's heart. He had one shot but I knew that would be enough and an inch to either side would still be fatal.

Then he went blind as a searing light erupted almost directly in front of him.

Zzzzzp.

"Oh dear, I'm so sorry," Marlene said by way of an apology as she walked out of her own temporary Time Portal. "I sometimes forget how powerful the ultraviolet light is on this thing. The permanent ones are quite dim in comparison, which I always think is a bit of a blessing in confined spaces. Everyone okay?"

Schwartz was still shielding his eyes and moaning, while the rest of us who had been facing away from the Portal had almost recovered.

"I admit I did add a little something because if I

have to be frank, Mr Lewis, it looked on my PortalVision as though you could do with a hand towards the end."

Lewis, Bryn, and Neets stared at Marlene in disbelief, whereas I'd had a pretty good idea she was going to arrive roughly when she did. After all I'd visited Marlene and arranged most of it. Inspector Smollett stood beside me looking nervous, then lingered by the Portal archway for a few seconds when he thought no one was looking before joining the rest of us. Schwartz's sight was beginning to recover, but Lewis had already taken away his sword and spare pistol as well as searched him for any other hidden weapons. The bald giant looked around with a sneer.

"So you've all come to see which one of us dies and which one takes over Port Eynon. Mind you, until you arrived through this Portal I had no idea how I'd get back to Camelot, but I understand this one will do it nicely thanks to the wonderful Merlin." As he talked, Schwartz moved slowly towards the Portal and then when no more than six feet from it he dived headlong through the archway and disappeared.

Zzzzzp.

Lewis swore, using words that even Neets and I hadn't heard before, then sprinted into action and was about to follow the wrecker in an equally impressive dive when my Inspector Smollett moved like a greased copper to stand in his way. With his right hand held forward, palm out, in the best traditions of traffic policing he took a deep breath because this was his moment; this was why he was a member of the Temporal Detective Agency and three hundred years from home. "I'm sorry, sir. I must forbid you access!" said the inspector. "The Portal is temporarily out of bounds." He stood his ground in front of the charging Lewis, looking massively relieved that he'd delivered his message.

Marlene tutted. "I wondered if he'd get it right, but you delivered the message Mr Inspector exactly as I told you to and right on time as well."

"Why can't I go after him?" asked a frustrated Lewis.

"Because before I came here Tertia told the inspector to change the dial settings to a new set of coordinates as soon as I arrived. Instead of taking you to another time, the Portal is now programmed to keep whoever enters in a sort of Limbo between all times, and there's no way out."

"But why didn't you warn me before?"

"Partly because you would have forgotten in the heat of the moment anyway, but mostly because I needed Schwartz to go to Limbo and for you to stay here."

"So what happens now?" said Lewis. "Do we all go home as though nothing has happened? What about the captain and his men over there? They'll have seen everything and it'll be the talk of Port Eynon by tonight." The Redcoats were staring with determined fascination.

"They'll forget about the whole thing in a day or two and so will history. Mark my words, the fact that a time machine, a wizard witch, her two apprentices, and some people from a Welsh seaside village were involved in the capture of the Black Knight from Camelot by Sir Gawain, also known as the White Knight," Marlene took a breath, "will never be remembered. Besides, I have a feeling something rather special is about to happen here."

The ultraviolet archway began to glow brightly and as it started to hum Lewis ran forward with his sword drawn in case Schwartz had managed to somehow return.

"Don't worry," said Marlene, "Put away your sword. It's not the wrecker, but I do believe it might be someone else you know."

The hum built to a peak as a horse trotted out of the archway coming to a halt in front of Lewis. A figure was half sitting, half lying in the saddle with its arms wrapped around the horse's neck and although the figure's eyes were closed and hair covered most of its face, I could see that Lewis knew who the rider was. He lifted the semi-conscious person off the horse and held her gently, staring in disbelief at his wife.

"Marie!" He spoke so quietly that the rest of us barely heard. "You're alive?" After all these years they were the most wonderful words he could say.

Marie Lewis didn't open her eyes. She was safe,

probably knew she was with her husband and slept with a smile.

"I think we ought to get back to Port Eynon," said Marlene. "There's nothing more to be done in this place."

"You knew Marie would be here?" asked a dazed Lewis as he carried her towards the Portal. "You knew my wife was alive?"

"No, not for sure, but when Tertia brought me Schwartz's journal we both began to suspect she might not be dead, which is pretty much the same thing. Come on, I'll explain it all later." She shooed us all into the Portal after carefully resetting the dials for the Lewis mansion cellars.

Zzzzzp.

As I walked into the Portal I waved to the Redcoats who saluted a fond farewell and more than likely forgot all about time travel and ultraviolet archways, because life is complicated enough anyway.

Chapter Fourteen

Marie's Story and Nelson's Return

Marie Lewis was sound asleep.

In fact she'd slept for nearly twenty-four hours with her family taking turns to sit with her in case she woke up or cried out in her sleep. Bryn stayed the longest, staring at the mother he'd lost when still a baby, usually with Neets sitting close by. He'd gently tried to wake her up a couple of times, but as Marlene assured everyone, sleep was the best medicine for what Marie had been through. That begged the question, what *had* she been through.

"Time is really weird," explained Marlene choosing her words carefully. We were in Lewis's study sitting in a semicircle round a roaring log fire. The lights were low and we all had something to drink; tea for most of us and a brandy for Lewis. "It doesn't just go forwards and backwards, it goes side to side and if you want it to, it just stops; a sort of neutral. I found out about the neutral bit by accident in the *Olé Grill* one day and I have to admit I found it quite spooky. It was me that called it Limbo."

"You said Schwartz is trapped there," said Lewis, "so how come you got out?"

"Good question. The answer is that I intended to go there and actually stopped Time from within the Portal while I was travelling with this little device." She held up what looked like a remote control with very few buttons and one dial. "From Limbo I could see everything that was going on, both from where I'd just left and where I was going and by really concentrating I could even see events in other Times. The only thing was that I couldn't go to any of them. I was stuck in Limbo, except of course I had the remote control so all I had to do was press the *on* button and off I went again. It can be a very lonely place because only one person can be in it at a time."

"But what made you think that my mum wasn't dead?" asked Bryn. "Her horse stampeded over the cliff and into the sea during a storm. We know that."

"No, Bryn, you were *told* that," I said. "Nobody I

met actually saw Marie's horse bolt, but rumours and hearsay became fact over the years. As a detective I find that if there's no body then it's often best to start with the assumption that nobody's dead!"

"She's right, Bryn," agreed Lewis. "I searched up and down the coast for days hoping to get word of Marie, or at least find her body, but there was no sign of her or her horse and one or the other should have been washed up somewhere along the coast."

"Absolutely. Then it occurred to me that if Marie hadn't died then the only person who would have profited from making you think she had was Schwartz. And if that was the case then he had to keep her in a place she wouldn't be discovered and couldn't escape from. That way he'd always have a hold over you."

Lewis was beginning to get the hang of the trickier parts of Time Travel. "You're saying that when you tricked Schwartz into jumping into the Portal you'd already set the controls for Limbo and knew he would be replacing my Marie?"

"No. Inspector Smollett set the controls and with his authority as a copper had to deliver the warning message to stop you entering. If I'd stood in your way you'd have just barged past me." Lewis nodded. "Anyway, because the Limbo control had been set from outside the Portal, whoever next used it would be stuck there with a one-way ticket."

"And my mum, did you know she'd come out of

the Portal when she did?"

"It was a pretty good bet, Bryn," said Marlene. "I was fairly certain by now she was being held in Limbo and that Schwartz would replace her. Luckily I was right."

"But what if you'd been wrong?" asked Lewis with just a tiny hint of menace.

"I wasn't, but if I had been then we'd still have trapped Schwartz," Marlene pointed out. "I was right and, Mr Lewis, you have your wife. Bryn, you have your mother. And, ladies, you have your sister back. So we're all winners." The Jones sisters smiled.

"Especially me," said Marie Lewis from the doorway. "It's good to be home."

She looked a bit frail, I thought, though for someone who'd lived in Time Limbo for around sixteen years she also looked pretty good. Nothing that a visit to the local hairdresser wouldn't put right, if they have such things in 1734. Her closest family ran to Marie, fussing round her and almost carrying the woman of the moment to a chair near the fire.

"I'm not ill," she laughed, "I'm just tired. I'll be as right as rain as soon as I've had a cup of tea and something to eat." Her face clouded slightly. "Then I suppose you'll all want to know how I disappeared and how I kept my sanity. But first some food and something to drink." She brightened again.

She wasn't exactly spoon-fed, but her older sister, otherwise known as the housekeeper Mrs Blodwyn

Jones, brought her a variety of delicious foods in several small dishes. "Not too much in one go, Marie," she said. "After all, you haven't eaten for sixteen years and you should never eat too much on an empty stomach."

Marie smiled as she ate slowly, watched attentively by her family and friends.

While Marie ate and got to know her family again, my Inspector Smollett and I returned to the twenty-first century. Lewis and his Redcoat brother-in-law had suggested that Inspector Smollett should take back the treasures Schwartz had stolen from the twentieth and twenty-first centuries and *discover* them, because shipping all the loot back and just dumping it would have been asking for trouble, and trying to put everything back where it came from would have taken years. So they reckoned this was the best solution all round. Let someone else do the donkey work – sorry, Pedro – and let Smollett take the credit.

Sorting out all Schwartz's plunder had taken ages and a large pile worth a small country had been set aside for my inspector. It now lay in a corner by Lewis's Time Portal and was ready to go with Smollett and me back to the future, so off we went.

Once back, the inspector decided to hold a press conference in a cave near Tunbridge Wells where he and I had apparently traced a gang of international art thieves, or at least all their treasure. Unfortunately the thieves had escaped, but the journalists had a field day talking to me, photographing the loot and making Inspector Smollett an instant hero. One journalist even asked whether I was the girl from the top of Nelson's Column and when I told him I was actually from Camelot and a qualified wizard – well almost – he got very huffy and flounced off. Some people don't know the truth when they see it and he had no idea how near he came to being turned into a rabbit.

That evening at a special ceremony Smollett was made a Chief Superintendent, I was made a fuss of, and then we both went back to Port Eynon because even my newly promoted Chief Superintendent wanted to hear Marie's story.

"I'm not sure what Schwartz intended," said Marie after she'd finished eating her first meal in years, "but far from trying to kill me, the night I disappeared in a way he actually saved my life. Did he have a first name by the way? If he did I never heard it."

"No, Marie," said Lewis. "He chose the name Schwartz because it means *black* and that was the colour of his heart. For sixteen years I've believed he killed you and to me he'll always be a murderer."

The looks on our faces said it all. We were all more than dubious about the wrecker's good side, even though I'd told them pretty much the same thing after reading his journal.

"Oh, I know it's difficult to believe," she said, "but it's true. I was riding back from visiting friends near

Rhossili and I decided to return along the headland. A silly thing to do I know, especially as it was obvious a storm was brewing, but I thought I'd get back in plenty of time and I knew the path well enough. I was making good time and had ridden past Mewslade when the wind picked up and the rain started. I suppose I should have dismounted and walked, but I wanted to get home to my husband and baby." She paused. "Could I have another cup of tea, dear?"

Blodwyn Jones motioned to Neets who hurried off to the kitchens and returned with a steaming cup. She had no intention of missing any part of Marie's story.

"Lovely. You've no idea how good a cup of tea tastes after all this time." She put the cup and saucer down. "I was just going past Paviland when I saw a beacon on the headland and knew it had to belong to the wreckers. Nobody in their right mind would put one there unless they wanted to bring ships onto the rocks." She touched her husband's hand. "I decided to find out for myself before telling you, dear, just to make sure. After all it might have been a false alarm. Unfortunately, it wasn't and I was soon surrounded by Schwartz's thugs." She sipped her tea.

"Just his thugs?" said Lewis. "Wasn't Schwartz there himself?"

"Oh he was there, though he kept in the background so I didn't see him at first. Mind you I was trying to turn and gallop away, but some of the wreckers grabbed my horse's bridle and were trying to make me dismount. I managed to break away by using my whip, but they blocked the path, forcing me towards the cliff. Then I saw Schwartz."

"That would have terrified me," I said. "Weren't you scared?"

"Not at all, dear. You're Tertia aren't you?" said Marie with a bright smile. "My sister has told me what an excellent teacher you'll make and how the children love your stories. Come and sit beside me and I'll carry on. The exciting bit's about to start!"

We all leaned forward.

"I could see Schwartz standing by the cliff edge near a place I believe he called the Leap of Faith, but it was so dark and stormy I couldn't really see him clearly let alone beyond him. However, it looked as though he was standing in a sort of rainbow archway, except it had only one colour and that was a sort of vibrant purple. I saw him fiddling with something and then the wreckers started to shout and fire their guns in the air, scaring my horse and making it bolt straight for Schwartz. I couldn't control my terrified mare and Schwartz stepped aside at the last moment. It was then that I saw the cliff edge and the incredible drop to the rocks and sea below. I could see the spray and hear the waves crashing far below, but I also knew I couldn't stop and that I was going to die. Then I was falling through the coloured archway and everything went still. I was no longer on the cliff and there were no wreckers. In fact there was nothing."

"You're saying that Schwartz saved your life, Mum, by sending you through his Time Portal," said Bryn.

"He and his men drove my wife through the Portal like a lamb to the slaughter." Lewis was incensed. "It was no accident and certainly no act of kindness by Schwartz."

Marlene nodded in agreement. "That's what I thought probably happened, Marie. I couldn't see how you, an experienced horsewoman, would be careless enough to go near the cliff edge on such a bad night. I also didn't think Schwartz would have killed you. He's a nasty piece of work, but he's not stupid. You would have been found and the trail would have led back to him eventually. Besides, he supposedly loved you. A Time Portal was the obvious answer. I just wasn't sure at first whether he'd sent you to another time period or whether, like me, he'd discovered Time Limbo and sent you there."

"Well, I had no idea where I was, or how I was going to get out. I just knew I hadn't been dashed to pieces on the rocks."

"What was it like in there?" asked Neets with the sort of curiosity normally associated with me.

Marie thought for a bit. "For a start I didn't feel as though I had a body and yet I could see it and could also see my horse, but both were almost ghost-like. It was as though I was thinking things ought to be there and so they were. The other thing was Time. It didn't really seem to exist although I had a sense of Time passing, but not in months, or years … just as *time*."

"What could you see?" inquired Marlene.

"That was the strange thing. At first I could see nothing really, just myself and my horse as shapes in a sort of greenish mist. I could see Schwartz looking at me, or rather looking at the Portal archway and laughing. I didn't want to see him anymore after that, so amazingly he just disappeared. Then I found that if I concentrated I could see anything I wanted, as though I was looking at a moving painting."

"Ah, PortalVision!" said Marlene. "A little invention of mine. Sorry, do go on."

"I think you can guess what I looked at mostly. I saw my son growing up to became a young man and I watched my husband help the village establish itself. Above all I saw their sorrow and knew I hadn't been forgotten."

I couldn't help thinking that if ever there was a time for a group hug this was it, but Port Eynon people are obviously made of sterner stuff, which is probably why they just smiled at each other. Time for a group smile then.

"The only way I could guess how many years had passed was by watching my Bryn grow up," Marie continued, "but I think I'd have gone mad if I'd only watched my family and soon found that if I concentrated I could look into pretty well anywhere in Time I wanted."

"PortalVision again," Marlene said proudly. "I

really must get round to taking out the patent."

"I saw some amazing things, but of course I could do nothing to help events, or warn people of impending danger. I saw what looked like a castle with lots of knights."

"Camelot. I was there," said Neets holding up a hand. Bryn was holding onto the other one.

"I know, dear. I saw you. In fact at one time or another most of you seem to have been there."

"I wasn't there," muttered the newly promoted Chief Superintendent Smollett.

"You wouldn't have liked it, my friend," smiled Lewis. "Very muddy." He turned to his wife. "There's one thing I'm not sure about, Marie, I still remember you exactly as you were the day you disappeared. I'll never forget how you looked. And yet you now seem about five years older than you did then. No years older I could understand, or even sixteen years, but five seems strange."

"Perhaps I can answer that," said Marlene. "The Time Portal is a very weird device and it affects people in different ways. An old friend of mine, for instance, went through a Portal and changed from being a gaga old man to a young knight with long wavy hair. You, Marie, only aged the number of years you thought you were in Limbo, or thereabouts. You, Mr Lewis, have aged far less than the sixteen years you should have, although you probably haven't noticed. You've been through the Portal so many times it's kept you young, which doesn't happen to many people."

"Bottle it and sell it," I said and meant it.

"I wish I could, dear. The fantastic thing is that you both don't only look years younger than you really are, but you'll also live that much longer, just like my old friend."

"Are you saying we haven't lost sixteen years of being together?" said Lewis in surprise. "More like four or five years and the rest will be added on?"

"That's about the size of it."

"But what about Schwartz?" asked Bryn. "Won't the same thing that happened to Mum be happening to him, and won't he be looking for a way out?"

"Put yourself in his shoes," said the wizard. "Unlike Marie, he has no one to love and no one to love him. All he'll be able to do will be to watch other people and he won't be able to influence them or get involved in any way. For him that'll be the greatest punishment of all and I rather think the years will literally drag by. The one thing he could lose will be his sanity. As to him getting free, only the few of us in this room know about Time Limbo and the fact that to get him out someone else would have to take his place."

"I almost feel sorry for him," said Neets. Though after what Schwartz did to our families as the Black Knight I suspected the main word was *almost*.

"Then there's the fact that someone here was working for Schwartz." Marlene paused. "That's true isn't it, David?"

The kitchen boy spun round as though he'd been hit, but regained his composure almost immediately and the stupid grin creased his face once more. "I'm sorry I'm a bit slow and silly, Miss. I didn't understand everything you said." His strong country Welsh accent made him sound so innocent. "Shall I go and make some more tea and sandwiches?"

I could see Marie was about to say how nice that would be, but Marlene raised her hand. "No, that won't be necessary, David. I also think you're a lot cleverer than you make out. What is your last name? Does anyone here know?" There were lots of shrugs and head shakes. "That's what I thought, though I'd guess your full name is David Schwartz and that you're the wrecker's son."

David stared at Marlene and looked as though he was going to deny everything with a flood of indignant words. Then his face changed and dull friendliness became a look of determination.

"Like father, like son?" said Marlene.

David backed towards the door, hitting Bryn as he did so and grabbed Neets round the neck. "If anyone tries to stop me I'll hurt her." The words were tough, but I could hear a tremor in his voice. "It's not so much whether I've got the strength to do it, it's more whether I've got the guts."

Marlene had been searching in her pockets for something that wasn't there and should be. "Blimey! He's got the Time Limbo controller. He has to be

242

stopped or he'll swap Unita for his father."

David's back was against the closed door now and he glanced round for no more than a second to look for the handle, but that momentary fumble was enough. Bryn launched himself in a perfect rugby tackle at knee height, while I flew at Schwartz's son with nails that would have made a tiger proud. Lewis kicked the door closed, but what really stopped David in his tracks was the uppercut punch landed by Marie. The boy's eyes opened wide in surprise and then glazed over as he slumped unconscious to the floor.

"No one comes between my family and me. No one. Not anymore. And I consider everyone here family." The look on Marie's face left nobody in any doubt.

Marlene searched David for the Time Limbo device and found it hidden deep in his pocket, wrapped in a handkerchief.

"Are you going to destroy the damned thing?" asked Lewis.

"I thought about it, but that would condemn Schwartz to an eternity in Limbo with no possibility of getting out. I couldn't do that to anyone, not even him."

"So what are you going to do? You can't leave it lying around."

Marlene looked at the controller, turning it over in her hand before slipping it into one of her bottomless pockets. "I'm going to give it to the one person who I know is a better wizard than me. I'll get Merlin to take charge of it. It'll be safe with her."

Neets was nursing her neck and overplaying the pain just slightly for Bryn's benefit. "One thing I don't understand," she said throatily, *cough, cough,* "is what made you suspect David all of a sudden. I worked here with him and never thought he was anything other than a slightly dim kitchen boy."

"David started working here about four years ago," I said, taking over from Marlene, "and it was about then that every move Lewis and his men made went back to Schwartz. That's too much of a coincidence. Someone inside the house was obviously passing information to the wreckers and the only person really close enough to our Mr Lewis and not actually related to him was David. It all pointed to him and I was right. There's another thing – when Bryn and I escaped through the Portal and went back to the Agency, Schwartz opened the door to the cellar and nearly caught us as we left. How did he know the house would be empty and who let him in? It had to be David. When Neets, Bryn, and I arrived in the Lewis mansion in 1734 the only person in the house was David. It had to be him."

There was no round of applause, though there was a groan from David as he started to regain consciousness. Chief Superintendent Smollett leapt into action, putting him in handcuffs before he could move a muscle. He even read him his rights, though I wasn't sure how valid they would be in 1734, but I bet it made my copper feel useful.

Now as we all know, there always has to be a final mystery.

There has to be something that everyone's forgotten about and this time it was my newly promoted Chief Superintendent Smollett who remembered that Marble Arch disappeared on the same day as Nelson's statue.

It's not easy to hide something so big and made of so much stone. The best place is always among a load of other massive archways, which is exactly where Marlene found it. The wizard reasoned that it had to be near a Time Portal, or at least where one had been and that it shouldn't look out of place, so in all probability it wasn't in Sherwood Forest. She found it tucked away at the back of a Hollywood film lot in the year 1924, but that didn't solve the problem of how to get it back to London a hundred years in the future without being noticed and without the help of a heavy gang.

"Think why it got where it did," I said helpfully. "It sort of got dragged there because the statue winged its way into Merlin's old cave and I got dumped on top of its column. Somehow Marble Arch got caught up in it all. I'm already here, so I reckon if you send back Nelson, Marble Arch will go back of its own accord. Sorted!"

We were sitting in the garden of Lewis's mansion enjoying both a late afternoon tea and the view stretching down to the sweeping sands that led to the rocky headland. It had been a good day and it seemed the right time to round off the case of the Leap of Faith.

"Very logical," said Marlene, "but how?"

"I think we have to do everything in reverse," said Neets. "Bryn started the whole thing in motion by setting off his father's Time Portal, which was focused on the statue because his dad was checking on the diamond. For some reason when Bryn started the device Marble Arch got sucked in as well as Nelson's statue and was sent somewhere it wouldn't be out of place. Ancient Rome would have been good, but Hollywood was easier and nobody would spot an extra archway there."

Marlene was sceptical. "So you're saying all we have to do is send the statue back and everything will return to normal?"

"Probably precisely!" said Neets cheerfully. I was beginning to wonder if she was getting over Bryn. She was starting to sound almost normal.

"Trust me, Marlene," I said, "this girl is on a roll. She's met the man of her dreams ... well, boy of her dreams ... and he seems to like her too. This girl can do no wrong!"

"You're both forgetting one thing," said the wizard. "Nelson's statue has an eye-patch and underneath it is

246

one of the world's most fabulous and valuable diamonds, stolen by our Mr Lewis to stop Schwartz from stealing it, if that makes sense. In real life of course Nelson never wore an eye-patch. So think on this, if he goes back on his column without an eye-patch people are going to notice. And if we take away the Koh-i-noor diamond we're left with two problems."

Lewis smiled. "Only two? I can see the biggest problem will be getting the diamond back into the Tower of London. After I stole it – though I'd much rather say that I removed it for safe keeping – I convinced the Tower authorities to move the Crown Jewels into a much more secure environment, which they did. That's why Schwartz couldn't even steal my fake. Returning it now will be pretty well impossible and if you're thinking of going back in time before the jewels were moved then you'll like as not replace the real diamond with the real diamond, which could be very confusing."

"So we leave the Koh-i-noor where it is in Nelson's eye?" said Marlene.

Lewis shrugged. "Why not? It'll be safe enough stuck up there, which was always my intention and no one will ever be any the wiser."

"We will," said Marlene, "but we'll have to live with it I suppose. Girls, it's time to put your theory to the test. Mr Lewis, take us to your Portal if you wouldn't mind."

We got up from the garden table and made our way into the house, down to the cellars and grouped together in the last room where Lewis's Time Portal was humming quietly to itself. Bryn and I walked forward and with Marlene's help programmed the dials before walking separately into the Portal and disappearing.

Zzzzzp. Zzzzzp.

Seconds later we both returned and gave a thumbs up. Marlene then set the dials to exactly the coordinates Bryn had used when he and I had first met, and stood back.

"Right, you two, you started all this, so it's only fair you finish it. Do the honours, Bryn."

"Where did you go, Tersh," hissed Unita as she watched her hunk walk up to the Portal.

"Back to Merl's cave to set the Portal dials and warn Galahad what was going to happen. Bryn went to Schwartz's place to do the same." I didn't mention that as I zoomed down the Time tunnel towards Merl's cave I saw Galahad feather-dusting Nelson's statue and rearranging the menus in the crook of the Admiral's arm. I also saw him examine the eye patch, prodding it with a finger, then examine it closer and give a chuckle. I couldn't see what he did next, but whatever it was he did it with a teaspoon and an even louder chuckle. When I arrived he had that look that said he was amazingly guilty of something and became quite flustered when I told him what we were about to do.

"So what *is* going to happen?" asked Neets. "Everyone seems to know except me."

"Watch."

Bryn pushed the switch to start the Portal and then walked back to rejoin us. Without thinking he took hold of Neets's hand and she let him. I nudged Marlene and smiled as the Portal hum grew louder and the archway took on the familiar ultraviolet glow, though it seemed to be brighter than normal and the hum much louder. Everyone was tempted to close their eyes and cover their ears, but what they saw next was worth the noise and bright lights.

The inner area of the Portal archway began to form a mist and then took on a milky whiteness as images began to flit across the PortalVision screen.

"That was Schwartz," said Lewis as the wrecker's irate face briefly appeared.

"Not a happy man." Marlene looked at me. I was trembling. "What's wrong, dear? Why are you pulling?"

"I'm not. It's the Portal, it's dragging me in!" I was clutching at Marlene's robes, but my feet were still sliding across the floor towards the archway faster than I could scrabble backwards. "Marlene, help!" I disappeared with a…

Zzzzzp.

I looked around. I was back in Trafalgar Square up on the column thing, which just goes to show you can't keep a good girl down, which also goes to show that relief often makes bad puns. I fished in the depths of one of my pockets and along with various invaluable oddments found an old tin cup. I put it to my mouth and spoke.

"Hallo, Marlene. Is that you?"

"Yes. Is that you, Tertia?"

"Of course it is! Who else is going to use an old teacup to let you know they're okay and standing on top of Nelson's Column again? I'm fine and ... *Wow*!"

I disappeared as fast as I'd arrived and was pretty sure I flew past Nelson's statue on its way back to the column where it belonged. The whole thing was working in reverse and I hoped I was on my way back to Merlin's cave to enjoy a nourishing and very expensive *Olé Grill* meal. I was half right.

When I stepped out of the Portal into the restaurant, Galahad was still looking anxious and desperately trying to hide something in his waistcoat pocket. The fact he didn't try to charge me for anything set alarm bells ringing and it only took seconds to get him to spill the beans, providing I promised I wouldn't tell a soul. I set the Portal controls for Port Eynon.

Zzzzzp.

It was good to be back. I was winded and sat down on one of the old packing cases for a quick breather because all this super-fast time travel is shattering even for a fit young detective and nearly-wizard like me.

"Why wasn't I sucked in as well?" asked Bryn and I had to admit it was a damned good question, one I didn't have an answer for and hadn't really given any thought to. I pretended Bryn's question wasn't addressed to me and looked at Marlene for inspiration.

"Oh, that's easy. You weren't part of the original swap, dear," said Marlene without a moment's hesitation. "You were just responsible for it. Anyway, there's one more little matter that's got to be sorted. Watch."

The PortalVision moved to concentrate on two holes on the ground. They were rectangular, close together and were empty for no more than a second or two as a massive structure zoomed from Hollywood to fill them. Marble Arch was back in place and because it was night time in London hardly anyone saw it happen and those who did probably had other things to think about, like walking in a straight line.

"It's over," said Marlene with a smile.

"For us, I think it could just be beginning." Marie squeezed her husband's hand.

Chapter Fifteen

David's Story, a Recruit and
Going Home

"Hands up everyone who would like Miss Tertia to stay." Miss Jones started to count but gave up when she realised every child in the school had no intention of letting me leave. At least not just yet.

I'd gone down to the school minutes after Marble Arch left Hollywood and for the rest of the day I stood in front of my class with Miss Jones, much to the delight of the kids, and I told them more stories about my adventures, especially about what had happened after Schwartz fell over the Leap of Faith. What's more I didn't exaggerate at all, because for once in my life I didn't need to. Boasting aside, I was a natural storyteller with the rare ability of making learning interesting and I loved doing it.

"Will you stay with us?" asked Miss Jones, "I'm sure we'd all benefit from your experiences and I know the children would love to show you round our Gower coast, especially those bits where you haven't been tied up, nearly drowned, or taken by donkey through a raging storm. We actually get quite nice weather down here most of the time."

I'd already decided that a week or two in Port Eynon would be the ideal opportunity to work on my tan. Besides, I couldn't see Neets wanting to leave Bryn for the joys of Merl's cave and the missing cats and dogs of the Temporal Detective Agency for a very long time to come.

Marlene was having great fun going through the parish records and piecing together the history of the village. She occasionally nipped forward in time and had a number of interesting chats with the Port Eynon vicar in the twenty-first century who also happened to be a Lewis. Marlene and I couldn't help wondering if Bryn and Neets were distant ancestors of his and half the village. Only time and a DNA test would tell.

Marlene was happy.

Lewis promised Marie he would never travel in

time again and she promised never to ride a horse at night unless he was with her and even then only on roads. He had also taken out his old Camelot clothes from the wardrobe and burned them with great ceremony in one of the headland beacons. As the fabric caught fire and smouldered into ash it was as though the past seventeen years had never happened and a whole chapter of his life had been wiped away, leaving him to enjoy the future with his wife and son. However, he did keep the Black Knight's helmet for use as a coal scuttle.

Marlene suggested that when she, Neets, and I eventually returned home Lewis should brick up the Time Portal and seal it in the cellar room to prevent anyone using it. Over the years people would forget why the last room was smaller than the rest.

Bryn and Neets spent every second in each other's company and I didn't spy on them once. I did stumble across them, though not quite literally, when taking the kids on a walk one day. They were holding hands and staring dreamily into nothing on one of the more remote beaches, so I deftly guided my class in the opposite direction to save my cousin's blushes. Neets was smitten big time and it looked to me as though I wasn't going to lose a cousin so much as gain a Bryn.

Chief Superintendent Smollett made up for all the rainy holidays he'd ever had and sat in a chair in the garden, sunbathing. If it got any warmer I reckoned he might even take off his raincoat.

I looked at the boy sitting in front of me and felt quite sorry for him. "Do you mind if I talk to you?" David Schwartz shook his head and stared at the ground. "I don't want to say anything nasty, but I had a friend once who had the same problem as you."

David looked up. "Problem?"

I sat down next to him. "So they put you in the stocks then. It could have been a lot worse I suppose." David's legs were secured by two wooden bars leaving him able to sit on a small stool with his arms free to shield himself from the fruit that people had thrown, which now littered the area. "At least they've given you plenty to eat!"

"Yeah, but I'd give anything for a good juicy steak to go with the veg." We both smiled briefly. It broke the ice. "Tell me about your friend."

"She was the daughter of a famous lady near where I come from and her father was a druid here in Wales. The lady was kidnapped and forced to marry someone else, a mighty lord, while the druid was imprisoned to keep him out the way." I decided to keep secret the identities of my friends Arthur, Guinevere, and her lover secret. After all it was the story that mattered, not the names, and David probably wouldn't have believed me anyway. "The druid enrolled his daughter into Merlin's academy intending that she would act as his spy in the enemy camp. We didn't guess for ages that she was his daughter."

"And when you did it was too late?"

"No. She'd spent most of her time trying to stop her dad and all his plotting, but without much success. In the end she helped save him from Arthur's vengeance and they all lived happily ever after back in Wales as far as I know."

"We didn't," said David as he chewed on a carrot. "I tried to help my dad and he ended up stranded in Time, while I'm a laughing stock."

"Why didn't you try to stop your dad?"

"I did, but you met him. He was always pretty ruthless even before he came to Port Eynon. Besides, he wasn't my real dad. I was washed up from a wreck and he decided to keep me, in case I was useful I suspect."

I thought back to the Black Knight who'd tried to overthrow Camelot. People didn't come more ruthless than that.

"And people don't argue with my dad ... not twice anyway. So when he told me to be a kitchen boy in Mr Lewis's house and feed him back information, I did as I was told. I didn't realise for a long time that by telling him where Mr Lewis and his men would be on a particular night a ship would be wrecked and sailors killed. I thought he was just a smuggler and once I found out what he was really like, it was too late. I just kept on getting the information for him."

"Surely you could have stopped? Maybe you could have just been a servant for the Lewis household and forgotten all about your father."

"He'd have come after me and I'd have gone over his Leap of Faith. I even tried giving him the wrong information, but most times it made no difference because he had other people in Mr Lewis's house on his payroll."

I picked up an apple, polishing it against my robes before taking a bite. I picked up another and handed it to David because all the better fruit was out of his reach.

"But then why did you grab Neets and try to set Schwartz free?"

David threw his apple core across the village square narrowly missing a passing dog that cocked its leg in protest. He shrugged. "A spur of the moment thing. He's my dad. He may not have been a great family man, but he was still the only dad I knew and I couldn't let him rot forever in the Time Limbo place."

I thought for a moment then nodded in agreement. He had a point.

"As to your friend Unita, I'm sorry but she was the nearest person at hand and if I was to get out of the room and down to the cellar I needed a hostage. Believe me, though, I wouldn't have hurt her, well certainly not intentionally. I just wanted to help my dad."

"That's what I thought. If I'm right you're also a pretty good shot with a musket." It was a bit of a stab in the dark, but I was fairly sure I was right. "It was you that fired that shot at Schwartz when he was going to stab Lewis at the Leap of Faith, wasn't it?"

David stared at me in surprise. "Yes, but how could you have known?"

"None of us had a musket and there were no Redcoats within a mile or so, plus of course whoever fired the shot stayed well away instead of making themselves known. You were the only person I couldn't account for and I was already pretty sure there was more to you than met the eye."

"Mr Lewis was always good to me and I wasn't going to let my dad kill him in cold blood so I followed you all and fired the musket as a sort of warning rather than anything else. It was only loaded with rock salt."

The more I talked to David, the more sympathetic I felt. It can't have been easy being Schwartz's adopted son. "After all that's happened and what you tried to do a couple of days ago, the Lewis household couldn't just welcome you back with open arms. Let's face it that's why you're in the stocks eating fruit and veg, but it's also why I'm going to make you an offer."

David looked dubious. "Offer?"

"The partners in the Temporal Detective Agency, that's me, Neets – sorry, I mean Unita – and Marlene, have got together and decided to make you an offer, which could work out rather well for everyone." It took seconds for David to accept our proposal as well as the restrictions that went with it, none of which were too tough. I unlocked the stocks' padlock and helped the newest member of the Temporal Detective Agency get to his feet.

The *Olé Grill* restaurant had closed for the night and Galahad was sitting at a table busily totting up the night's taking. We'd all just arrived through the Time Portal and were sipping Merl Grey tea and nibbling extremely expensive biscuits, although Galahad had mumbled *on the house* with extreme difficulty and a stammer.

My Chief Superintendent Smollett had already made his farewells to take even more credit for recovering Nelson's statue and somehow returning Marble Arch to its rightful place. He always reckoned for that lot he should have been made Assistant Commissioner at least, but as he refused to tell anyone how he got a statue onto a hundred-and-fifty-foot high column and several tons of stone into Hyde Park he decided to let the matter drop.

David was given a position in the Temporal Detective Agency for as long as he wanted on the understanding he would only go back to Port Eynon when Lewis and Marie weren't around. After all, he'd proven he was pretty good at surveillance work and it was time to put that skill to good use for a change.

The most difficult parting was between Bryn and Neets.

On the day fixed for returning to the *Olé Grill* the

young couple had walked for miles along the coastline talking incessantly and learning even more about each other than they already knew, which was nearly everything. Neets told me they talked about Bryn going back with her to Merl's cave, but they both agreed that now Marie had returned he had to stay with his family. Neets suggested she could stay in Port Eynon, but the thought of leaving Marlene and me as well as all her cats and friends from Camelot was more than she could bear. They agonised all day and eventually came to a heartrending decision just as it was time to leave and for the Time Portal to be bricked up almost permanently. They agreed that Neets would pop back to see Bryn the following day using a portable Portal and he would go forward in time the day after that by the same means. Temporal dating can be so difficult for teenagers.

Galahad finished counting and poured himself a flagon of mead because Camelot habits die hard. With a sigh he looked at the large palm bush that now stood where Nelson's statue had become a favourite conversation piece and told me its disappearance had left him with two problems. Firstly, he'd had to buy a very ordinary looking rack to put his menus in, which for a celebrity chef was a bit of an indignity. Secondly, and probably more important, he had no idea what he was going to do with the great big diamond he'd found under Nelson's eye patch, though cut properly it would make a nice tiepin and cufflink set for him and a not too ostentatious pendant for me. He hadn't meant to keep it of course, but the statue had suddenly disappeared and my two-minute warning had given him no chance to put the stone back, let alone the eye patch. Meanwhile, it would be safe in the tea caddy and the hardboiled egg he'd put in the statue's eye socket would almost certainly never be discovered.

Marlene's office wall had always looked a bit bare with a very noticeable and unsightly damp area. As a sort of farewell present Lewis had given her a portrait of a woman painted on a piece of wood that now covered the patch perfectly. The copy was in the Louvre in Paris, but somehow I didn't think Leonardo da Vinci would mind, after all he hadn't even bothered to paint the *Mona Lisa* on canvas.

Marlene looked at her little band as we made ourselves at home. She smiled with satisfaction and settled back in her easy chair, because everything had gone rather well, all things considered.

Neets had grown into a young woman, had a young man in tow and yet she and I seemed closer than ever. We were Merl's Girls after all. I was officially guest teacher at Port Eynon Junior High School and was now considering writing a textbook on my experiences. I already had the title, *Tertia's Cylcepodica,* and Marlene reckoned it could be the first book to be published simultaneously in a number of different centuries and languages. She also knew from her researches in the future parish records that Lewis would lead a long and healthy life in Port Eynon, though even with all the parish records at her disposal she hadn't managed to find out whether Neets played a greater part in creating the Lewis family tree, but then some mysteries are best left unsolved. For the time being at least.

Then of course there was David.

He was certainly smart, definitely sneaky enough for the Agency and best of all he and I got on. From David's point of view staying in Port Eynon would have been impossible. He would have been an outcast and would probably have been forced out of the area anyway. Best of all he'd be able to watch his father through PortalVision and one day Marlene was sure they would be able to release him, but not for a long time yet.

Marlene picked up the battered tin cup and spoke quietly into it. "Merlin? Hallo, it's Marlene. Just touching base as it were. Can you hear me?"

There was a muffled crackling like tissue paper being crumpled and then a voice came from a long way away, or at least a thousand years in the past.

"Marlene! Lovely to hear from you. How is everybody?"

"We're fine, Merl. We've just had a lovely holiday and solved a mystery or two. The girls are fine and Galahad's making a fortune. How's Arthur?"

"Oh, he's Arthur. Still my lovely Arthur, still king,

and we're both very happy. In fact I haven't told him yet, but I think there could be a little prince on the way."

I could hear the excitement in Merl's voice. "Merlin, that's wonderful news! I always wanted to be an auntie."

There was a pause.

"Are you busy at the moment, Marlene?" Something in Merl's voice said this was more than an idle query. "It's nothing major you understand. It's just that Camelot's having a few problems at the moment. Conspiracies, marauding knights, and some say the odd dragon apparently. We're going to see what we can do, but we're a bit stuck, because to top it all someone's stolen Excalibur and without the Sword we're helpless. You and the Agency couldn't help out, could you?"

I grinned. We were going home to do business and this time we might even get paid, which made it the best combination of all. Though this was royalty we were talking about and they never have ready cash.

Next day out of curiosity I looked through PortalVision.

High up on the top of Marble Arch a puzzled workman, found a Sioux arrow and what was definitely desert sand. While nearby in Trafalgar Square the sun glinted off the boiled egg that replaced the statue's right eye. Neither the pigeons, nor Nelson seemed at all worried that

Galahad had a nice new pair of cufflinks, I had a pendant and that hundreds of people queued every day to see the fake Koh-i-noor diamond in the Tower of London.

After all, it was only a Leap of Faith.

THE END

Great Authors

Meet Authors Reach authors and discover our books:

- Detective Thrillers
- Paranormal
- Horror
- ChicLit
- Fantasy
- Young Adult

Visit us at:
www.authorsreach.co.uk

Join us on facebook:
www.facebook.com/authorsreach